SUMMER

She heard footsteps
quickened. She hope
regretted hoping. Sl materialized in the gray haze.

It definitely wasn't Diver.

"I come bearing the gift of muffins."

It was Austin, holding up a white paper bag. Summer's heart fluttered.

He looked pretty much the way he had when she'd first met him on her flight to Florida over Spring break: tattered jeans jacket, worn jeans, a couple of tiny silver hoops in one ear. He had submitted to a haircut, she could tell, but his dark brown hair was still operating by its own rules. He hadn't shaved in at least a week, though his faded T-shirt was wrinkle-free, a concession, she supposed, to her.

"May I come up?"

Summer gave a small nod. She did not like what she was feeling – tingling skin and liquid bones and a stomach freed from gravity, the kinds of symptoms generally associated with the early stages of the flu. The symptoms she remembered from her early days with Seth.

They were not feelings she wanted to be having. She told herself to stop having them.

She was not listening.

Titles in the MAKING WAVES series

1. Summer can't choose
2. Seth wants more
3. Diana fights back
4. Marquez breaks free
5. Summer's last chance
6. Diana makes a move

More books in this fabulous new series will follow soon!

MAKING WAVES

Summer's last chance

KATHERINE APPLEGATE

Pan Books

Cover photography by Jutte Klee

First published 1996 in the United States by Pocket Books

This edition published 1996 by Macmillan Children's Books
a division of Macmillan Publishers Limited
25 Eccleston Place, London SW1W 9NF
and Basingstoke

Associated companies throughout the world

ISBN 0 330 34951 1

1 3 5 7 9 8 6 4 2

A CIP catalogue record for this book is available from
the British Library.

Printed by Mackays of Chatham PLC, Kent

For Michael

1

The Magic of Prom Night and Other True Myths

The doorbell rang at seven o'clock on the night of Summer Smith's senior prom. While Summer's mother ran to the door with her camera in tow, Summer stood calmly at the top of the stairs.

Wiser, worldly girls with diplomas and cars of their own had told Summer what to expect from her senior prom. In all her years of high school, they vowed, nothing would be as magical. Not homecoming, not the Christmas dance, not senior skip day, not the day she cleaned out the banana peels from the bottom of her locker for the very last time. Not even the great moment when the principal handed Summer her diploma. Nothing could compare to senior prom, these girls claimed. Things *happened* that night.

But Summer suspected that senior prom was just another high school ritual, even if it did feature giant paper pom-poms and boys in pastel cummerbunds. It was just a dance, just a corsage, just a chance to play dress-up. Not magic.

She'd even considered skipping the whole expensive event, since Seth, her boyfriend, lived far away. Besides, her good friend Jennifer was in a temporary state of guylessness, and it seemed only right not to go. Solidarity and all.

But in the end, Seth had convinced Summer that, as an official senior, it was her obligation to attend the prom. And Jennifer had promised that she was not going to slit her wrists just because she had to miss some stupid dance.

She glanced down at her long black velvet dress, sleek and sophisticated, slit to the thigh in a style that was both sexy and very practical for dancing. Her blond hair was swept up in a simple French twist. Her mother, with some trepidation, had lent Summer her diamond earrings and pendant. Jennifer had helped her do her nails and even her toenails. Summer was wearing her favorite perfume, a fresh, lemony scent that reminded her of Florida, where she'd first met Seth.

Her mother opened the door, and there stood Seth, looking impossibly older and grave in a formfitting black tux. He gazed at her and blinked.

"You look . . . so beautiful," he whispered in a voice full of sheer amazement.

"You look . . . so beautiful, too," Summer said, and then she laughed.

Her mother snapped a million or so pictures of Seth pinning on Summer's corsage while he tried very hard not to touch anything off-limits. Out the living room window, Summer could see a black stretch limo filled with their friends waiting at the end of the driveway.

Seth took her arm.

He said it again: "You look so beautiful."

It was an I-can't-believe-my-eyes kind of voice.

And for the first time Summer wondered if maybe those older, wiser girls had been right after all.

2

Pen Pals at a Prom Are Not a Pretty Picture

So what if the crepe paper in the Hyatt ballroom kept falling on the dancers? So what if the band played Nine Inch Nails—badly—whenever the chaperons sneaked outside for a cigarette break? So what if the punch tasted remarkably like Gatorade?

None of that mattered. It was still incredibly romantic.

Except for one tiny little nagging detail.

Summer laid her head on Seth's shoulder as they swayed slowly to the band's cover of "I Will Always Love You." She tried to concentrate on the feel of his arms around her. She tried very hard not to think about the letter in her purse that was threatening to ruin her entire evening.

If only she hadn't seen it as she and Seth were walking out the door, she'd be dancing in blissful ignorance. But no, Summer *had* noticed the envelope addressed to her in the pile of mail on the hall table. She'd seen the return address. She'd seen the name Austin Shaw. And after considering whether to faint or not, she'd grabbed the note and stuffed it in her purse while Seth was busy promising Summer's mom he would behave himself that night.

As she danced, Summer once again told herself not to overreact. It was probably just a "Hi, what's up, drop me a line sometime" note. The kind of letter a friend wrote to another friend.

Only Austin wasn't exactly a friend.

Summer put her arms around Seth a little tighter. He hated to dance, but he was pretty good at it. She rubbed her cheek on the stiff, cool fabric of his tux and closed her eyes.

She and Seth had been together almost a year. Like all couples, they'd had their ups and downs. There'd been jealousies and misunderstandings the past summer. During the school year, with Summer living in Minnesota and Seth in Wisconsin, there'd been too-quick weekend visits and too-long phone calls.

And over spring break, when Summer and Seth and their friends had spent the week on a yacht in Florida, there'd been . . . well, complications. Complications of the male variety, which Summer didn't like to dwell on.

The point was, she was there with Seth at that moment, and all was well. Better than well.

It was just a letter, nothing more.

"What?" Seth whispered in her ear, sending a shiver down her spine.

"Did I say something?" Summer asked, loudly enough to be heard over the wailing lead singer.

"You sighed."

"Oh." Summer gazed up at him. "I was just thinking about how much we've been through."

"It's been worth it, though." Seth stroked her hair gently. "And now it'll start to get easier. We'll have the end of the summer in Florida, and then college together in Wisconsin." He grinned. "And after that, who knows?"

The song ended, but couples still swayed lazily. Seth leaned down and kissed Summer for a wonderfully long time.

"Let's go outside," he whispered. "There's something I've been meaning to ask you."

"What?" Summer asked.

"Wait till we're outside," Seth said with a mysterious smile.

She took his hand as they drifted off the dance floor and past the long table filled with cookies and a big plastic punch bowl. Parents stationed behind the table watched them pass with discreetly approving smiles.

"I have to go pee," Summer said.

"I'll wait with the other abandoned males," Seth said, nodding toward the group of guys waiting patiently near the ladies' room.

"Don't let her go," a guy in a red cummerbund warned. "She'll never come back. It's like the Bermuda Triangle in there."

The rest room was packed with girls adjusting straps, bemoaning runs, retouching blush, respraying hair.

"Please, Summer, save me." Mindy Burke grabbed Summer by the shoulders. "Please tell me you have some deodorant in your purse."

Summer held up her tiny beaded black purse as evidence. "Does this look like it could hold anything?" she asked.

"Perfume?" Mindy pleaded. "I'll take anything. I can't believe I've been planning for this prom for, like, decades, and I forget my deodorant. I am such an idiot. Anyone have any perfume? Hair spray?"

"Please, Mindy, tell me you're not going to use hair spray on your pits," someone groaned.

When she reached a stall at last, Summer locked the door. The air was thick with mingled perfumes. She opened her little beaded purse. It was hardly worth carrying—she'd barely managed to fit a comb, a quarter, and a box of Tic Tacs into it.

And, of course, Austin's letter.

Austin T. Shaw, read the small print in the left corner of the envelope. It spoke to her like a voice, like *his* voice—soft and caressing and full of trouble.

She pulled out the letter. Notebook paper, torn on one edge. A coffee stain on the bottom.

Her hands were trembling, and she didn't know why.

May 14

Summer, my beautiful, unforgettable Summer. Of course you are surprised to hear from me. Probably as surprised as I am to be writing you.

I know I left you abruptly in the middle of your spring break with nothing but a scribbled letter, a pair of mouse ears from Disney World, and, undoubtedly, a lot of questions.

I'm writing to tell you that I have discovered some of the answers.

I told myself I left you because I was afraid. Afraid of hurting you. Afraid of getting involved when I knew I might have inherited my father's nightmare, the awful disease that is stealing his life away.

But now I wonder if maybe I wasn't

also afraid of what I was feeling for you, it was so intense and complete. And although I might have been able to handle it, I wasn't so sure you could. Not when you still had feelings, as you obviously did, for Seth.

On one score, at least, I can stop being afraid. It seems I have some good news and some bad news. The good news: I had the genetic testing done and I'm clean. I won't get Huntington's like my dad did. The great gene lottery smiled on me. I don't know why me and not my brother. I've stopped asking, because I never seem to be able to come up with an answer.

Summer closed her eyes. She felt tears coming. Her mascara was supposed to be waterproof, but she couldn't afford to take the chance. She took a couple of deep breaths.

Someone pounded on the door. "Did you fall in or what?"

"Just a second," Summer said. Her voice was quavering. She found her place in the letter.

Anyway (and this is the bad news, although I hope you see it differently), I'm going to reappear in your life and further complicate it.

I can't stop thinking about the feel of your mouth on mine. I can't stop thinking about the way you felt in my arms. I want to be a writer, so why can't I find a way to put my feelings about you into words?

I know you said you're heading down to Crab Claw Key after graduation. I'll be there, waiting, whether you want me to or not.

I remain hopelessly in love with you.

Austin

Summer took a shuddery breath. She folded up the letter neatly and put the little square into her purse.

"Summer, you okay in there?"

"I'm fine," Summer called.

She'd thought she had put Austin out of her mind. Well, not out of her mind, exactly. He appeared in her dreams with startling regularity. But out of her heart, at least.

She'd chalked him up as a spring fling, a momentary slip. He'd been a stranger in need of help, a guy about to visit his very sick father and perhaps learn that he too was destined to be very sick. She'd been a good friend.

A good friend who couldn't seem to stop kissing him.

Seth had found out about them in the worst

possible way. He'd seen them together, and he'd made accusations she couldn't deny.

Eventually, though, he'd forgiven her. She didn't deserve his forgiveness, but he'd given it willingly. She'd been so grateful to Seth for a second chance to make things work.

Diana, Summer's cousin, had warned Summer that if she didn't get her priorities straight, she was going to lose Seth to someone who appreciated how wonderful he was. And Marquez, Summer's best friend from Florida, had told her the same thing.

They were right, of course. Seth was wonderful.

And if Austin was wonderful, too, in different ways, well, that really wasn't the point, was it?

With a sigh, Summer unlocked the door and made her way through the crowd.

"Turns out hair spray does not make a good deodorant," Mindy reported. "My pits are, like, permanently attached to my dress." She peered doubtfully at Summer. "What's wrong with you? Someone die?"

"Someone's *not* dying, actually," Summer said.

She captured a place at the crowded mirror.

Her mascara was definitely not waterproof.

3

I Dos and I Don't Knows

Behind the hotel was an enclosed courtyard with a pool and a Jacuzzi. Seth led Summer to a pair of chairs near the pool. Austin's letter sat in her dainty little purse like a slowly ticking bomb.

Why did the existence of that note make her want to confess to sins she hadn't even committed? After all, during spring break Summer had told Seth the truth—that she'd had real feelings for Austin, and that if he hadn't left so suddenly, she wasn't sure what she would have done. She'd been honest. Belatedly, but still, that counted for something.

So why did she feel so guilty now, because of a single piece of coffee-stained notebook paper?

Seth glanced around, then cleared his throat.

The wide patio was empty. A soft, cool breeze rustled the trees. The moon shimmered on the surface of the turquoise pool.

"It's not exactly the ocean," he apologized, "but it'll have to do."

"Seth," Summer asked, "is something wrong?"

"Nothing's wrong. As a matter of fact, everything's perfect. I just want it to stay that way."

"So do I."

"Have I told you in the last two minutes how beautiful you are tonight?" Seth whispered.

"You look pretty great yourself. This tux thing is good on you."

"Maybe I could get a job at a fancy restaurant, wear one all the time."

"It wouldn't be the same covered with mustard stains."

Seth grinned. "I can tell you're an ex-waitress. You think you'll work at the Crab 'n' Conch again when you go back to the Keys?"

"The Cramp 'n' Croak? I don't know. It wasn't exactly fulfilling, but the tips were good."

Summer sighed. Soon, very soon, she'd be back in Florida for the summer. She couldn't think about it without recalling Austin's promise—or was it a threat?

I'll be there, waiting, whether you want me

to or not. I remain hopelessly in love with you.

"Well, if Marquez is working with you at the Cramp," Seth said, "you'll have a lot of fun, even if it isn't the most fulfilling job on earth."

"We can't all have big la-di-da internships like certain people."

Seth smiled. "They can call it an internship all they want. I'm still going to be just another boat grunt."

"A boat grunt building ultralight racing sailboats," Summer corrected. "It beats the heck out of asking 'Do you want fries or coleslaw with that?' a hundred million times." She squeezed his hand. "You should be really proud, Seth. They had dozens of applicants for that internship."

"I know. It's just that it means I'll be separated from you for part of the summer. California is so far away." He gazed off at the pool. Yellow lights glowed beneath the surface like the eyes of great fish. "Before long, you're going to be back on Crab Claw Key hanging out with Diana and Marquez just like last summer. I can't imagine not being there with you. And . . ."

"And?" Summer prompted.

"And I'm not sure I can stand being apart. I know we'll be going to college together next fall, but still . . . it seems like such a long time."

Summer nodded. Three months and then college with Seth. It didn't seem like such a long time, really. They'd decided on the University of Wisconsin together. Seth wanted to go to college where his father and grandfather had gone. Summer hadn't felt strongly about a particular school as long as she and Seth could be together. She'd applied to some other colleges, even a difficult liberal arts school down in Florida, but in the end Wisconsin had seemed like a good compromise.

"Three months isn't so long," Summer assured him.

Seth's deep brown eyes were filled with longing and worry. "I just want to know we'll always be there for each other."

"Of course we will be, Seth," Summer whispered. "You know I love you." And if not so long ago I thought maybe I loved Austin, too . . . well, that's over with, she added silently. Forgotten.

Seth nodded. "I also know I almost lost you over spring break."

"Just because I had feelings for someone else doesn't mean I'm not totally in love with you."

"I know that," Seth said. "People can have feelings for more than one person at a time."

Something in his voice told her he really understood. It was strange, the way he was capable of putting himself in her place so easily. Sometimes she almost wished he'd been angrier about Austin, less understanding. It would have made the guilt easier to bear.

"What happened over spring break made me realize how important you are to my life, Summer. And, well . . . I know this is, like, the corniest thing in the world to pull, but here goes."

Seth reached into his jacket pocket and removed a small black velvet box.

Instantly Summer knew what it was. She stopped breathing. Before she could sort through all her panicky reactions, Seth was down on one knee.

"God, I feel like such a dork," he said. "But you gotta do these things right."

When Summer opened her mouth to speak, he hushed her, placing a finger over her lips. "Before you go into logic overdrive, hear me out, okay?"

She nodded. Her heart was sprinting madly in her chest, but she kept her face expressionless.

Carefully Seth opened the little box. A small diamond on a simple gold band caught the moonlight.

He took her hand. "Look, I know that it would be absolutely and completely crazy for us to get married now. I *know* that, I really do. Maybe it's even crazy to get engaged now, but—" Seth gave a helpless, endearing shrug. "I guess I just don't care. Sometimes you do the stupid, crazy thing."

He caught Summer's surprised look and laughed. "Okay, so that's not the first thing you'd expect to hear from a guy who color-codes his sock drawer. But I just *know* in my gut this is the right thing for us, Summer. It doesn't mean we'd have to get married right away. I mean, I think we should finish college first, don't you?"

Summer moved her head slightly. It was not really a nod, just an acknowledgment of the question.

"All I want this to be is a private symbol between you and me that says we love each other and we always will."

Summer stared at the ring. Her mother's ring looked just like this one. Small. Simple. Her mother hadn't really wanted to bother with it, she'd told Summer. She hadn't needed a symbol, hadn't wanted to waste the money. Summer's dad had bought one anyway.

And now her parents were separated. Her dad lived in an apartment near his office. He used plastic spoons and forks from take-out places. The empty rooms echoed when you walked through them.

Her mother slept in the guest bedroom now. At dinnertime she kept forgetting not to set a place for Summer's dad.

Carefully Seth removed the ring from its little box. "Summer?" His voice was trembling. "Will you marry me?" He looked up at her and smiled. "Someday?"

Before she could answer, he slipped the ring onto her left ring finger. It was a little tight, and he had to push to get it past her knuckle. But there it was, shiny and important. It felt heavy on her hand.

The ring glimmered, a seductive promise. It was simple and easy.

It promised that even though her parents had messed up, and even though she'd messed up with Austin, things didn't always have to be that way. It promised that it would always be there, a tight gold reminder on her finger, making life easy just as she was heading out into the big, cold world.

It promised that sometimes it was okay just to do the stupid, crazy thing.

It promised to make Austin go away.

"Summer?" Seth whispered. "Will you?"

She looked at Seth with tears in her eyes. When she tried to say yes, no sound came out, so she had to nod instead.

4

Crab Claw Key, Florida. There's No Place Like Home. Sort Of.

"Welcome home, engaged person."

Summer's cousin Diana swung the door to the stilt house wide open. It creaked loudly, just as it always had.

Summer stepped inside, set down her bags, and breathed deeply. The Florida air was thick and hot, like steam from a teapot. It carried a hauntingly familiar scent, part mildew, part salty ocean tang, part rotting wood, part sweet hibiscus. Not a great smell, some people would say. But to Summer, it was CK One and Love's Baby Soft and Chanel No. 5 all rolled into one. It was her signature scent: Stilt House No. 1.

She'd spent the previous summer there, sharing the space with Diver, her brother, and a territorial pelican named Frank, and although she didn't own the place (her aunt Mallory did), Summer thought of it as her own. The little bungalow was a squat and homely affair, but it was a historical landmark of sorts—rum smugglers had used it during Prohibition in the 1920s. The building sat above the water on wooden stilts. A rickety walkway wrapped around the house, then ran a hundred feet back to the grassy shore. Beyond that sat the huge home where Diana and her mother lived.

"A plant!" Summer exclaimed, noting the big philodendron on the middle of the wobbly kitchen table.

"From Mallory," Diana explained. She never called her mother Mom. "She had some other stuff done, too. New comforter on the bed, new silverware and glasses."

Summer opened the cupboard above the sink. "Matching glasses! No more Lion King and Slurpee cups. This is excellent."

"Well, you're practically a married woman now," Diana said, sitting on the bed in the far corner of the room. "Married women have utensils, Summer."

Diana kicked off her sandals and sat cross-legged on the bed. She looked as stunning as ever. Long dark hair, gray, unsettling eyes the color of the ocean on an overcast day. Although they were cousins, Diana had been adopted, a fact that always seemed embarrassingly obvious to Summer when they were together. Diana, who was a year older, exuded confidence like a character who'd walked off the set of *Melrose Place*. Which was not to say she hadn't had her share of troubles. Diana's confidence masked a tendency toward deep and dangerous depression.

"For the record, Diana," Summer said, "I am not practically married. Jeez, I just graduated from high school a few days ago."

"But you're wearing a rock on your left hand." Diana grinned. "Or should I say pebble?"

"I already told you." Summer plopped her suitcase onto the bed. "Seth and I are not engaged, exactly. We're more like . . . engaged to be engaged. Semiengaged."

"I don't think you can be semiengaged. It's like being semipregnant or a semivirgin." Diana eyed Summer up and down. "Hey, that isn't what's going on here, is—"

"Give me a break!" Summer groaned. "I am definitely *not* pregnant and definitely still virginal, not that it's any of your business."

"Maybe that was the idea, though." Diana wiggled her eyebrows suggestively. "Think maybe Sethie had ulterior motives? Figured if you're practically married, you'd say what the heck . . ."

"You've known Seth since he was a little

kid." Summer unzipped her suitcase. "What do you think?"

"No," Diana conceded, "that doesn't sound like Seth. He's the most wholesome, all-American guy I've ever met."

"You don't have to make him sound so boring."

"I don't think Seth is boring, Summer," Diana said. Her voice took on a strange, wistful tone. "I think he's pretty great, actually." She stood and went to the window. The drone of a motorboat filled the air. "That's why," Diana added, "I thought it was so odd, the call I got a couple of days ago."

Summer looked up, a bunch of T-shirts in her arms. "What phone call?"

Diana opened the little window over the kitchen sink, taking her time. She turned, shaking her head sorrowfully. "The phone call from Austin Shaw. The one telling me to pass along the message that he'd see you soon."

Summer dropped her shirts on the bed and closed her eyes.

"Summer, Summer, Summer." Diana clucked her tongue. "If we're going to be roommates soon, you have to keep me updated on your romantic escapades. How am I ever going to cover for you?"

"You don't need to cover for me."

"I did during spring break," Diana pointed

out. "After Seth found you and Austin in, shall we say, a compromising position, wasn't I the one who had to go around pretending Austin and I were hot for each other?" She sat on the bed and began carefully refolding one of Summer's T-shirts. "Not that it was such a terrible sacrifice, given that he bears a striking resemblance to Ethan Hawke. But it was kind of a waste of time, since Seth figured it all out anyway."

Summer looked at her cousin. "Diana, that is over," she said firmly. "Seth understands what happened. He forgave me." She shrugged. "And if Austin wants to try to get in touch with me, I can't exactly do anything about it, can I? What do you want me to do, get an unlisted phone number? Maybe I could go into the witness protection program, get a whole new identity."

"Okay, okay. Don't bite my head off."

"Sorry. I guess I'm just tired, after flying down and everything. I had graduation a few days ago, and then yesterday I saw Seth off to California. I feel like my entire life is changing, and I can't keep up with it."

"Have you talked to Seth since then?" Diana asked with interest.

"Last night. He said Newport Beach is great and he's really psyched about the boat building internship. But he wishes he were here."

"So do I," Diana said. She paused. "I mean, for your sake, it would have been great."

Summer sighed. "Come on." She pointed to the door. "I want to check out the view."

"Nothing's changed. Except I think that pelican of yours is actually fatter, if that's possible."

They stood on the weathered deck, leaning gently on the ancient railing. The small island was shaped much like a crab's claw, with the two "pincers" enclosing a sparkling expanse of turquoise water. Motorboats vied with sailboats and gulls for space on the little bay, and postcard-perfect palm trees hugged the shoreline.

Frank was perched on the railing. "Hey, Frank, remember me?" Summer asked.

He responded by pooping on the walkway, then eyeing both girls with obvious disdain.

"You two really have a rapport going," Diana commented.

"Frank was mostly Diver's friend."

"I guess you . . . haven't heard from Diver or anything?"

Summer shook her head.

"He and Marquez are pretty hot and heavy these days. You're bound to see him, you know."

"I know," Summer said softly.

Diana kicked at a loose railing. "You really could come stay up in the main house, Summer.

Mallory's in and out on book tours, and we have, like, a hundred extra rooms."

Summer glanced back at her aunt's ornate pastel house—the perfect dwelling for a successful romance novelist. "I like it here," she said.

Diana shuddered. "Roughing it. I just don't get it."

"It's not just that. This place has lots of memories."

"Well, pretty soon we'll find something cool for ourselves. I can't wait to move out of Mallory's." She nudged Summer. "Maybe you and I should scope stuff out, then let Marquez in on it. She has no taste."

"She just has wild, out-there taste."

"Like I said."

For a few moments they didn't speak. The waves lapped at the slick wooden stilts with gentle insistence. Summer hadn't realized how much she'd missed that soothing sound.

"Summer," Diana said, breaking the spell, "are you sure about Seth? Really sure?"

Summer looked out at the familiar, endless vista of blue-green waves. "I'm sure."

"How do you know?" Diana asked. "I mean, I'm not sure I've ever really been sure." The uncertainty in her voice was unnerving. Diana usually radiated confidence like a force field. "Sure enough to wear a ring like that one, anyway."

Summer hesitated. She and Diana, despite being cousins, were not that close. But it would be nice to confide in someone, and why not Diana? They were going to be roommates for the next three months. It wasn't as though Summer was going to have any secrets for long.

"The truth is," Summer said, choosing her words with care, "I don't know what 'sure' means, exactly. I just know that when I saw this ring, it made sense. I was feeling overwhelmed, I guess. You know, with graduation and college and my parents splitting up, it felt like the whole world had been turned upside down. And then I saw Seth holding this ring in the moonlight, and bam, everything was right side up again." She touched the little diamond. "It made all the pieces fit together. I could see my life, college and being with Seth and everything else, and it felt good, you know?"

Diana frowned. "So you got engaged because you were feeling confused? I'm not sure that qualifies as the best reason on earth, Summer."

"That's not the only reason," Summer protested, so loudly that Frank took off in a huff. "I love Seth. Totally."

Diana watched Frank resettle in a palm tree farther down the shore. "Sorry. I guess I just don't understand. But if you're happy, then I'm happy for you."

"I'm definitely happy."

"Yeah, one of those."

"You're not going anywhere near Newport Beach, are you?"

"There's a schedule Kara sent me on the table over there."

"Mind if I look?"

"Why? Are you and Summer planning a big party in my absence?"

Diana rifled through the mass of papers on the table. "Actually, I was thinking I might go with you." She located the itinerary. "Laguna Beach, Newport Beach, Long Beach, Los Angeles. Excellent. Mallory, how about a little quality mother-daughter time?"

"Why?"

"Why? Because we are mother and daughter. You wound me."

"Uh-huh. What gives?"

Diana patted her mother on the head. "You're going to the land of Rodeo Drive armed with credit cards, and you wonder why I want to come along?"

And if Diana just happened to stop by and say hello to Seth while she was in the neighborhood, so much the better. There was nothing wrong with a simple hello, was there? It would be an innocent get-together, nothing more.

Nothing at all like their not-so-innocent get-together last New Year's.

"Call Kara and she'll arrange the tickets."

"I'm not exactly sure yet," Diana said. "I have to wait and see how things go. It depends."

"On what?"

Diana shrugged. "Well, for one thing, I want to get things settled here with Summer. The apartment hunting and all that. I just want to make sure everything's definite."

Like which guy Summer's decided on, Diana added silently. Summer could deny it all she wanted, but Diana could tell she wasn't over Austin, not by a long shot.

It wasn't fair—not to Austin, not to Seth, and not to Diana.

A shudder ran through her as she remembered the way Seth had held her that New Year's night. Long months had passed since then, but she could still hear his whispered, hypnotic voice and feel his lips on hers.

She'd tried to let it go. She'd written him long, passionate, embarrassing letters, but she kept every one in a little cardboard box. She'd dialed his number on lonely nights, but she'd always hung up at the sound of his voice. Out of a sense of loyalty and guilt, she'd even done her best to help get Seth and Summer back together.

But what exactly had her honorable intentions gotten her? Summer was halfheartedly engaged to Seth while still infatuated with Austin. And Diana was left out in the cold.

She headed off to the kitchen. "Want some chocolate-chip cookies? It's a much more direct route to inner peace."

5

Ex-boyfriends and Ex-brothers

"Sunscreen, Dr. Pepper, beach towel, romance novel, sunglasses, Blistex, brush."

Summer surveyed her beach bag with satisfaction. After nine long months of Minnesota weather, it was nice to get back to the basics. She consulted the mirror in her bathroom. The two-piece bathing suit she'd bought to wear over spring break still fit, more or less.

She checked the clock on the ancient stove. Diana would be waiting for her up at the main house. Well, she could wait another minute or two.

Summer grabbed the phone book from the kitchen cupboard. It was tiny compared to the fat white pages back in Bloomington. But as she'd hoped, Aunt Mallory had supplied her with the newest edition, hot off the presses.

She sat at the kitchen table, turned to the *S*'s, and scanned. *Samuel, Sandía, Smal.* Nope, back a little.

Shaw, Aaron M.

Shaw, Augusta.

Shaw, Carl.

Summer breathed a sigh of relief. No *Shaw, Austin.* Could be he hadn't moved down there after all. Could be he'd been calling from Missouri, where his family lived.

Could be he was living a couple of blocks down the street and he'd just gotten his phone the week before.

Summer closed the phone book with a groan. Maybe she'd call information later. Maybe not.

Maybe, when you felt the hand of fate swooping down at you, it was better not to know exactly when or where it was going to hit.

"Can you believe it? Here we are, just like last summer," Marquez exclaimed. "Only Summer's wearing an engagement ring, I'm about to be the first person in my family to graduate from high school, and Diana . . ." She sat up on her beach towel and lowered her shades. "Well, Diana's leaving her coffin much more frequently these days."

"One other change," Summer noted. "You

have lost so much weight, Marquez. You look fantastic."

"Fantastic as in 'Marquez was such a whale before, and now she looks more like, say, a manatee'?" Marquez asked. "Or fantastic as in 'Marquez was such a pig before, and now she looks like, say, Ms. Slender Teen Cuban-American of Crab Claw Key'?"

"How about second runner-up?" Diana suggested.

Marquez tossed a handful of sand at her. "It's not like I'm fishing for compliments, exactly. It's just that after J.T. broke up with me, I felt like such a complete loser, and now I'm starting to feel like the new, improved Maria Marquez."

"How did you do it?" Summer asked. "You've lost a *lot* of weight, Marquez."

"I know." Marquez laughed with pleasure. "I look down at my thighs sometimes and I think, whoa, somebody call the cops and file a missing-person report."

"But how?" Summer persisted.

Marquez shrugged. "Running on the beach, mostly. Plus my neighbor was throwing away her old exercise bike, so I grabbed it out of the trash. That's cool, because you can exercise while you watch Letterman."

"You exercise that late?" Summer asked.

"She exercises constantly," Diana said, with that hint of disapproval that always ticked off

Marquez.

"Way to be sensitive," Marquez said, rolling her eyes. "I'm cursed with fat-thigh genes. Some of us have a lonely battle to wage."

Diana flipped the page of her newspaper, fighting the ocean breeze. "I just think you're getting a little obsessed, that's all."

"I wouldn't expect you to understand, Diana. You're the only person I know who can eat an entire pound cake and actually *lose* a pound." Marquez shook her legs. There was still a trace of cellulite here and there. Another inch gone would be nice. Two would be better.

"Well, I'm very proud of you," Summer said.

Marquez grinned. Man, it was nice to have Summer back. Diana was the kind of friend who took work. She was critical and just a little too smart for her own good. Not that Summer wasn't smart, too—but she had the good sense to accept you the way you were, no questions asked. She was the perfect hanging-around, all-purpose best friend.

Diana held up her yellow highlighter in triumph. "I've found it! Listen to this." She folded her newspaper and marked an ad. " 'Three-bedroom, two-bath charmer on Coconut Key, ocean view, beach access, Jacuzzi, pets okay.' "

"How much?" Summer asked eagerly.

Diana cleared her throat. "Twenty-two hundred."

"A *month?*" Summer cried. "That's, like, my entire income last summer waiting tables."

Diana shrugged. "I was just fantasizing. Okay, so we'll downsize a little."

"Try a lot," Marquez advised.

"How many bedrooms?" Diana asked. "Maybe we should we get extra for visitors." She cast a grin at Summer. "What if Seth and Austin show up at the same time? We'll need extra room, won't we, Summer? Or at least a very big bed."

"Austin?" Marquez repeated.

"He's ba-aack!" Diana said. "He wrote Summer. He called Summer. And he promised to see Summer very soon."

Marquez grabbed Summer's arm. "You *are* kidding! The same Austin Shaw who almost caused you to break up with Seth?"

"Yes, that would be the one," Summer replied dryly. "Now can we drop it?"

"Right. You know me better than that."

Summer reached for her sunscreen and recoated her arms. "I believe we were discussing our apartment," she said, sending Diana and Marquez a frosty look.

Marquez knew what that look meant: Let it go for a while. Fine, she could take a hint. But one way or another she'd get the truth out of Summer eventually.

"It should be quaint," Summer continued.

"I want my first real apartment to be something I'll remember forever." She paused. "Of course, in a way the stilt house is my first official apartment."

"Doesn't count," Diana said, tapping her highlighter against the paper. "It's your aunt's." She frowned. "You know, Mallory did say we could live at our house this summer, but I told her we wanted to suffer."

"Let me get this straight." Marquez sat up. "You said no to a free gigantic house with big-screen TV and a billion bedrooms?"

"Don't forget the espresso maker," Diana said.

"I hate espresso. But I love money, and this could save us a bundle."

"Marquez," Diana said reasonably, "Mallory would be there. A maternal unit would be living in your midst."

"Yeah, I see your point. She is a little nutty."

"She's way past nutty. She's trail mix. She's—"

"Okay, we'll rent." Marquez didn't want to get into that again. Diana was very generous with her money, which she had way too much of. But she just didn't get *not* having money. It wasn't that she was insensitive, exactly. It just didn't occur to Diana that not everybody's mother was a best-selling novelist who drove a Mercedes.

And really, Mallory wasn't so bad. Or was it the

fact that Marquez's parents were moving to Texas the day after next that made having a mom around seem tolerable? It was fine to complain about your mom, until you started thinking about what it would be like not to have her around to complain about.

"Marquez?" Summer asked. "You okay?"

Marquez adjusted her sunglasses. "Me? Yeah. Hey, I'm about to be an official graduate of John F. Kennedy High. Of course I'm okay. I'm way okay."

Diana rolled onto her side, observing Marquez with that annoying look that made Marquez feel as though her head were transparent. "Wasn't there something you wanted to discuss with Summer?" she said pointedly.

"You know, it's not like I've ever had trouble moving my mouth, Diana."

"You get no argument here," Diana said. She jerked her head at Summer.

"What?" Summer said. "Tell me, Marquez."

Marquez stared off at the ocean. A gang of seagulls was squawking uproariously over some shared bird joke. Laughing gulls, they were called. Summer's brother had taught her that. Diver knew all about birds and animals.

Summer nudged Marquez with her foot. "What, Marquez?"

"It's about Diver," Diana said softly.

Marquez took a deep breath. "See, the thing

is, Summer, with you coming to my graduation tomorrow . . ." This was way too hard. Marquez hated getting stuck in the middle of other people's problems. But there she was, stuck big-time.

"You want to know about Diver." Summer bit her lip. "If I'll be okay if he comes, too."

Marquez nodded. "If you don't want him there, he's really cool with it. He understands. I mean, he's the one who ran out on your family. He's the one who's been holed up here in Florida for the last few months."

"It's fine, Marquez." Summer smiled, but Marquez could see the effort that went into it. "I wouldn't ruin your graduation for anything."

"And the party at my house after," Diana prodded. "He'll be there, too, Summer."

"It's okay," Summer said, more insistently this time.

"I was a little worried," Marquez admitted, "when you went to talk to him over spring break and didn't go through with it."

"It wasn't the right time," Summer said flatly.

"And now it is?" Marquez pressed.

"It'll have to be."

"He misses you, you know."

"I guess he should have thought of that before running out." Summer's voice was biting.

"Still, it'll be great having you both there tomorrow," Marquez said soothingly.

"I wish Diver could have been there for mine." Summer gave a tense smile. "It was hard. My mom and dad didn't even sit together."

Marquez played with the edge of her beach towel. She knew Summer blamed Diver for their parents' separation. Wrongly, Marquez felt, but she wasn't about to tell Summer that. The girl was bummed enough.

The laughing gulls were sniping at each other, nipping at feathers as they fought over a piece of seaweed. This wasn't going to be easy, dating Summer's brother while living with Summer. It was going to make Marquez the go-between and conciliator. The UN of the Smith family.

Marquez groaned. Could World War III be far off?

6

A Big Day for Marquez, a Bad Day for Summer

"There she is," Diana whispered. "Our little graduate."

Summer and Diana waved frantically from their seats in the bleachers. Marquez waved back.

John F. Kennedy High was a much smaller school than Summer's, and its size translated into a much more informal graduation ceremony. For one thing, it was being held outside, on the football field, while Summer's had been inside the cavernous gymnasium. For another, this was Florida, and it was nearly ninety-two degrees outside. That meant the assembled spectators were dressed in Crab Claw casual: shorts, T-shirts, even bathing suits.

By comparison, Summer, in her ribbed blue

tank dress with a straw belt, was dressed up. Diana was wearing a denim miniskirt with a halter top. But the rest of Marquez's family, her parents and five brothers, were wearing their stiff Sunday best. This was a big occasion for them. Marquez's parents had come to the U.S. from Cuba when Marquez was just a little girl. They'd had nothing but the clothes on their backs and their hopes.

"You must be very proud of Marquez," Summer said to Mrs. Marquez.

"Look at her sitting there, so serious," her mother said with a laugh. She had the same huge eyes, naturally olive complexion, and dark tangle of curls as her daughter. "You'd think she was going to the dentist."

"Maybe she's worried about Diver showing up," Diana pointed out.

Summer glanced down the bleacher rows. Still no sign of her brother. She felt a terrible mixture of relief and sorrow. She knew how much Marquez wanted to have Diver there that day. But Summer really didn't want to face her brother, not yet.

She'd tried over spring break. She'd gone to the wildlife sanctuary where Diver lived and worked. She'd come within a few feet of him. But the words just hadn't been there.

Diana nudged her. Marquez's mom and dad were kissing and whispering. Summer fingered her diamond ring. They looked so happy. Was it possible to stay in love when you were old enough to have a daughter graduating from high school? Summer's parents hadn't.

True, Summer's mom and dad had suffered in ways most parents only had nightmares about. Diver had been kidnapped from them as a child. And when he'd finally been reunited with them, the strain had been more than he could handle. He'd left after only a few months of halfhearted effort and returned to Florida.

And after he was gone, the fights between Summer's parents had begun. "It's your fault for pushing him too hard." "It's your fault for not pushing hard enough." "If only you'd tried harder." Each whispered accusation was another broken thread, until the whole fabric of Summer's life had unraveled before her eyes. The week before Summer left for the Keys, her mother had set up an appointment with a divorce lawyer.

A small woman bustled onto the dais and tapped the microphone. "Welcome, friends and family of our wonderful graduating seniors!" she exclaimed. She went on to extol the virtues of the graduating class. They were the adults of the future, the hope of tomorrow, the shining beacons in a troubled world.

Listening to the familiar words, Summer found it hard to believe she herself was a high school graduate. In three short months she would be a real, live college student at the University of Wisconsin. It seemed impossible.

She tried to imagine herself walking to class with Seth past the pretty brick campus buildings she'd visited earlier that year, but the image wouldn't stick. It didn't feel like *her* school, not the way Bloomington High had seemed like her personal campus by the time she was a senior.

Sometimes she imagined herself on another college campus—Carlson, the one in Florida that her English teacher had encouraged her to apply to. She'd been accepted, but Seth hadn't, and that had pretty much ended that discussion. Besides, it had been just a whim. It was a tough school, too rigorous for Summer. She would never survive the academic competition. And of course she wouldn't dream of going to college without Seth.

Diana nudged her. She pointed to the football field.

Striding across it toward the bleachers was Summer's brother. His hair was a shimmering sun-streaked blond, his tan dark. He scanned the bleachers with intense blue eyes.

His gaze locked on Summer, and her heart stuttered. He didn't smile or turn away. He just looked at her with his open, hopeful, accepting, beautiful face.

She wanted to do something, maybe wave or

smile. But she just sat there, stunned, frozen by old pain.

Slowly Diver made his way up the crowded bleachers until he came to Marquez's family. He took a seat at the other end, as far as he could get from Summer and Diana.

Marquez saw him and gave a little wave. He waved back, grinning broadly. He did not look at Summer again.

Summer couldn't help looking at him, though. He was wearing the suit her parents had bought for his halfhearted job-hunting efforts back in Minnesota. He'd refused to wear it, saying it cramped his style and that if he couldn't get a job wearing jeans, he didn't want a job. There'd been a fight about it, a long one. Summer had taken her dinner to her room that evening to avoid the sharp words.

And now there he was, in ninety-plus degree heat and humidity that would wilt a piece of steel, and he was wearing the stupid suit.

Sure, he could wear it there, then, when it didn't matter anymore.

When it was too late for her parents to see it.

"They make a cute couple, don't they?" Diana said early that evening.

Summer nodded sullenly. Marquez and Diver did look great together as they danced on the Olans' wide, sloping lawn. The graduation party was in full swing, packed with Marquez's classmates and family members. A popular local band played on the patio. Mallory had called in her favorite caterer to provide the food. Colorful Japanese lanterns swayed from the trees in the twilight, and tiki torches burned at the edge of the water.

"We're starting to get party crashers," Diana said, noting the swelling crowd.

"This is probably the best graduation party on the key," Summer pointed out. "Marquez is really grateful that you went to all this trouble."

Diana shrugged. "You know Mallory. Any excuse for a party—and she adores Marquez." She sipped from a paper cup of lemonade. "Still, it would be nice if Marquez could at least say thanks."

"I think money stuff is kind of tough for her. Her parents lost the gas station, and now they're moving. She's not even sure she can swing college tuition."

Diana nodded distractedly. "Speaking of tough situations," she said, eyeing Summer, "you haven't said two words to Diver yet, have you?"

"I haven't said one word. It's like we're invisible to each other. Which is fine by me." Summer winced at the anger in her voice.

"Uh-oh. Mallory's waving me over. That

can only mean a catering crisis." Diana brushed off her skirt. "Want to come?"

"Yeah, I'd be a lot of help in a catering emergency." Summer rolled her eyes. "We don't have caterers in Bloomington. We just nuke some Jeno's pizza rolls and call it a day. I'm going down to the stilt house to change into some shorts."

"You're not going to hole up and pout, are you?"

Summer pretended indignation. "I'm a high school graduate. High school graduates do not pout."

"Nobody ever told *me* that."

"It's at the bottom of your diploma, in really fine print," Summer said.

She crossed the wooden walkway to the stilt house. With each step the raucous music and swell of voices receded a little. The truth was, she *did* want to hole up in her house until the party ended—or at least until Diver left. But how long could she keep that up? What was she going to do when she and Diana and Marquez got a place together? Ban Diver? Lock herself in the bathroom every time he showed up?

"Hey, Frank." The pelican was sitting on the railing near her front door. He blinked and fluttered a wing.

Inside the stilt house, the music was just a throbbing bass line, like rhythmic thunder. The kitchen was cool and shadowy. Summer didn't turn on any lights.

On the kitchen table, the little yellow Post-it note sat like an accusation. Her aunt Mallory's scribbled, cryptic message was barely legible. When Summer had found it that afternoon after the graduation ceremony, it had taken her a minute to decipher her aunt's shorthand: *Austin cld. Cn't wat 2 C U. No #.* She was grateful, at least, that Aunt Mallory hadn't made an issue of it in front of Diana and Marquez.

It was too bad Austin hadn't left a number. It would have given Summer a chance to warn him off, to announce her engagement and send him on his way. Now she was stuck with this feeling of foreboding, waiting for the other shoe to drop.

She rifled through her ramshackle dresser, trying to locate her khaki shorts. In her new place, maybe she could have an actual closet of her own.

Suddenly she heard a gentle, tentative voice outside the open window.

"Hey, guy. Did you think I forgot you? Look, Frank. I scarfed you some anchovies."

Summer closed her eyes. Diver. Only he could be standing on her walkway, chatting with a pelican.

She crouched behind her dresser. Maybe he

didn't know she was there. Maybe she could keep it that way.

"I'll bet you're glad Summer's back, huh, Frank?"

From her position on the floor, she could just make out Diver's silhouette against the velvety purple sky. He had his back to the railing. His jacket was gone, and his tie hung loosely around his neck. He might or might not have been looking into her window. She couldn't be sure.

"We had a lot of good times here," Diver mused. Summer wondered whether he was talking to himself, to Frank, or to her. "Remember sitting on the roof, you and me and Summer, watching the sun come up? The whole sky was on fire."

Summer did remember. She remembered the way they'd sat together in silence, awed and humbled, like two lone visitors in the world's largest cathedral. Diver had been a mystery to her then, just as he still was.

"I miss this place," Diver said, almost whispering. He was peering through the window. "I miss you, too. And Summer. I miss her a lot."

Summer stifled a sob.

"I guess she's kind of mad at me. Not that I blame her."

Another sob, this one audible.

"Maybe if we could talk," Diver said. "Maybe I could explain."

Summer sniffled.

The door creaked. She saw two tan bare feet sticking out of black pants. She looked up.

Diver stood there in the shadows. His hand was out. He was holding a handkerchief.

Summer took it and blew her nose. She sniffled again.

Diver turned on the kitchen light, then straddled a chair.

She started to give the handkerchief back.

"It's Jack's. He gave it to me when he bought the suit." Summer sat very still on the floor, her back against the dresser. She looked at the handkerchief. In the glare of the overhead light, the white linen almost glowed. Her throat felt as though she'd swallowed gravel.

"Mom got a divorce lawyer," she said, twisting the handkerchief in her hands. She didn't look at Diver.

She waited for him to say "It's not my fault" or "So what?" She had answers for those words. She'd practiced them in her mind, all the angry things she would say to Diver when she finally had the chance.

"Because of me," he whispered. It wasn't a question. It was a statement of fact.

Summer looked up. Diver's face was expressionless.

"Why didn't you—" She choked back a sob. "Why didn't you stay, Diver? Why didn't you try a little harder to belong? The rest of us wanted so badly to make it work."

"Because I didn't," Diver said. "Belong. Because . . ." He opened his hands, palms up, as if he expected the right words to fall into them. "I knew I wasn't going to stay. I figured it was better to leave sooner rather than later. I didn't want you all getting more . . . attached."

"Attached?" Summer cried. "Attached? You're not some stray dog we picked up off the street. You're my brother, you're their son. Doesn't that mean anything to you?"

Her voice echoed in the little room. Diver folded his hands together. He thought for a long time. "I didn't have your life, Summer. To me, Jack and Kim are just nice people. I grew up with other, not-so-great parents. I didn't have your perfect life."

"Do you have any idea what it did to Mom and Dad to lose you? And then to . . . to find you again, to have you back in their lives, and just vanish again? You leave a note on my bed that says 'I'm sorry,' like that somehow evens the score?"

Summer realized her hands were shaking. She climbed to her feet, pacing back and forth to use up the wild energy fueling her anger. "After you left, it was nothing but Mom blaming Dad and Dad blaming Mom for not handling you better. Then it was like they got tired and gave up. Well, I blame *you,* Diver. It wasn't because Dad pushed you to get a job and Mom bugged you to cut your hair. It was *you.*"

She dropped onto her bed and bent over, burying her head in her hands.

After a moment Diver joined her. He touched her hair, then pulled his hand away. "It wasn't just the job, Summer," he said softly. "It was other things. They wanted me to tell them who my other parents were."

"You mean your kidnappers."

"I was only two, Summer. They were my parents to me." He sighed. "Jack and Kim wanted to press charges, to prosecute them."

Summer wiped her eyes. "And you have a problem with that?"

"I want to let it go."

"You want to let everything go, Diver. You just want to escape. You can't live your whole life that way."

Diver stood. "I guess it's the only way I know how."

He turned to leave. At the door he paused. "Keep the handkerchief. It's more yours than mine."

On the walkway, Summer heard him stop to talk to Frank, but she was sobbing too hard to hear what he said.

7

Up on the Roof

Summer awoke the next morning before dawn. She put on shorts and her blue and gold Property of Bloomington H.S. Athletic Dept. T-shirt and made herself a cup of herbal tea.

The air outside was cool and wet. The sun was just a secret, glowing on the horizon. Waves stroked the stilts beneath the house lazily.

Summer climbed up the ladder that led to the roof, the way she had the year before with Diver. The shingles were rough on her skin, like cats' tongues. She sat very still. Now and then she sipped her tea. But mostly she just sat and waited.

With Diver the previous summer, watching the dawn unfurl had been a wonderful moment.

Spiritual, almost. They had shared something too big for words.

She wished it had gone better with him the night before. She didn't regret what she'd said. In fact, she'd been relieved to finally cut loose and drop her anger at his feet. Maybe Marquez was right. Sometimes it did help to just go ahead and be angry, instead of tying your feelings up in polite little packages with pretty ribbons, the way Summer had learned to do.

But now she was left with a gaping hole where the anger had been. She felt diminished. Smaller than before. Watching Diver walk away, his shoulders sagging, she'd felt awful.

But what could she do? Pretend he hadn't failed her family? Pretend he hadn't hurt her?

She heard footsteps on the dock, and her pulse quickened. She hoped it was Diver, then instantly regretted hoping. Slowly a figure materialized in the gray haze.

It definitely wasn't Diver.

"I come bearing the gift of muffins."

It was Austin, holding up a white paper bag. Summer's heart fluttered.

He looked pretty much the way he had when she'd first met him on her flight to Florida over spring break: tattered jeans jacket, worn jeans, a couple of tiny silver hoops in one ear. He had submitted to a haircut, she could tell, but his dark brown hair was still operating by its own rules. He hadn't shaved in at least a week, though his faded T-shirt was wrinkle-free, a concession, she supposed, to her.

Austin was not the kind of guy you'd bring home to Mom. If Mom was feeling charitable, she might see a sensitive, tortured, down-at-the-heels poet. If she wasn't, she'd see her worst nightmare, the boy who was going to corrupt her innocent daughter and leave her broken-hearted.

"Austin." It was all Summer could think of to say.

He stood on the deck below her, gazing up in rapture as if he were having a religious moment.

"When I remembered your being this beautiful," he said, "I told myself I was crazy, no girl was that perfect. Now I see I was right all along." He grinned broadly. "Of course, when I imagined you, you were generally *in* a house, not on one. But what's a preposition in the grand scheme of things? May I come up?"

Summer gave a small nod. Austin tossed her the bag of muffins. They were still warm. She did not like what she was feeling—tingling skin and liquid bones and a stomach freed from gravity, the kinds of symptoms generally associated with the early stages of the flu. The symptoms she remembered from her early days with Seth.

They were not feelings she wanted to be

having. She told herself to stop having them.

She was not listening.

Austin crawled across the roof and settled next to her. The spot where his shoulder was touching hers burned.

"So," he said. "We meet again."

Summer hugged her knees and nodded.

"You haven't gone mute in the meantime?"

She shook her head. Her voice was lodged in her throat like a piece of hard candy. She didn't dare try it.

Austin turned to look at her. She could smell his shampoo, or his aftershave, or his deodorant—something, anyway, that was lime-scented and exotic.

"You got my messages?" he asked.

Summer nodded.

"And my letter?"

Another nod, this one conveying regret and annoyance, she hoped.

"And would it be out of line to wonder if you'd give me a hello kiss?"

This time the nod was vehement.

"I see."

She'd forgotten how compelling his voice was, how full of wild promises.

"Well, can you at least hand me the muffins?"

Summer did. Austin took one out. The fragrance of blueberries wafted through the air.

A coppery halo glowed on the horizon. Summer fixed her gaze on it. She practiced the words in her mind like lines in a play.

"I'm glad you're okay," she said at last.

This time it was Austin who didn't speak.

"I thought you were afraid to take the test," Summer said.

Austin stared at his muffin, a bemused look on his face. "I was. Scared like I've never been scared."

"What made you change your mind?"

"Something you said, actually."

"Me?"

Austin touched the back of her hand with his fingertips. "You asked what if I went through life assuming I was going to get my dad's disease, and it turned out I was wrong? Afraid to get involved with anyone, afraid to take the chance. It would just be so ironic. So I had the genetic testing done after all." Austin gazed out at the drowsy ocean. "And lo and behold, the gods smiled on me."

"What did your family say?"

"My mom was thrilled, my dad . . . well, he's too out of it to really understand, I'm afraid. My brother—"

"The one who tested positive for the gene?"

Austin nodded. "Yeah. He was really glad for me, but I could tell he was thinking, 'Why me and not him?' Which was pretty much what I was thinking. Life doesn't make a whole lot of sense sometimes." He turned to face her. "But that's something I'm starting to realize, Summer. Life doesn't always make a whole lot of sense. Sometimes we don't know exactly why we do what we do." He took her hand, but she slipped out of his grasp. "Which is why I've moved to the Keys."

Summer blinked. "You've moved to the Keys," she repeated very slowly, as if she were just learning English.

"I got a job waiting tables over on Coconut Key. You know, a little ways up the coast?"

Summer knew. It was one of the places Diana and Marquez wanted to go apartment hunting.

"Why are you doing this, Austin? Moving here, following me? You run off at spring break and tell me to have a nice life. You leave without any explanation—"

"Actually, I left a very articulate note," Austin interrupted. "Not to mention the photos from our Disney World trip."

"Without any explanation," Summer persisted, "and I get my life back together with Seth, and now you show up and go, 'Hey, by the way, my genes are okay, and I've decided to move in next door'?" She held out her left hand. The little diamond caught the faint pink morning rays. "Do you know what this is?"

"Cubic zirconia?"

"It's an engagement ring, Austin. Seth and I are engaged. Do you know what that means?"

"Um . . . I'm guessing I'm probably not invited to the bachelor party?"

Summer didn't smile.

Austin sighed. "I saw the ring right away, Summer, and yes, I know what it means. I just don't happen to care. Jewelry as an expression of commitment does not impress me. Besides, one thing a brush with mortality teaches you is to live for today."

"*Carpe diem,*" Summer said. "I remember."

He flashed her one of his most charming smiles. "Anyway, I happen to like it here. You've got sun and ocean and pelicans"—he gestured at Frank—"and I've got a job I can stand, and a not-too-bad apartment, except for the roaches you can saddle up and ride. Even without you, it's a nice place to be." He took her hand, covering the ring, and this time he wouldn't let go. "Of course, with you it would be perfect."

"There won't be any me."

"That's what you said on the Skyway to Tomorrowland at Disney World, and then you kissed me like I've never been kissed before."

"You must have had very limited kissing experience."

Austin leaned a little closer. "As it happens, I've had a lot of experience."

His lips were so close. The guilt and the recriminations evaporated. Even thoughts of Seth evaporated. All she felt was a terrific pull, as though she were a speck of steel and a million magnets were tugging her closer and closer.

"Just one kiss," Austin whispered, "for old times' sake."

Summer closed her eyes to the rosy horizon and Austin's dark gaze. She could feel her pulse throbbing through her temple like a marching band.

If she stopped thinking and just felt the pull, guiding her closer, it felt so sweet. It felt so good, so right, if she just didn't think. . . .

8

I Think We Have a Really Bad Connection. . . .

"You still there, Seth?" Diana asked as she headed toward the stilt house, phone in hand.

"I'm here."

"Sorry, I slipped and almost dropped the phone. The grass on the lawn is really wet."

She made her way down the sloping lawn. The dawn light cast long shadows. The yard was filled with the remains of Marquez's party: crumpled napkins, overflowing trash barrels, a discarded T-shirt, a pair of sandals, a handful of wet crackers.

"We had a great party last night," Diana said. "Very major. Wish you could have been here."

"Me, too," Seth said. His voice was fuzzy. The connection was pretty bad.

"What time is it there, anyway?" Diana asked.

"Way too early," Seth said. "I couldn't sleep."

"How come you're calling? Is anything wrong?"

"No . . . I just, you know, wanted to tell Summer hi and stuff. You know."

And stuff. "Yeah, I know." Diana's grip tightened on the phone.

"She doing okay? Summer, I mean?"

Diana stopped suddenly as the sloping roof of the stilt house came into view.

Well, well. What an interesting sight this was. Her little cousin on the roof, in what appeared to be a very passionate embrace with Austin Shaw.

"Diana?" Seth's voice was tinny and indistinct.

Diana put the receiver to her ear. "Yeah?"

"I said is Summer doing okay?"

"Oh, yeah. I'd say she's doing just fine, Seth. You don't have to worry about Summer. She can take care of herself."

She took a few steps onto the walkway that led to the stilt house, then held up the phone. "Summer!" she called.

Diana watched with grim satisfaction as Summer and Austin disentangled frantically.

"Diana?" Summer yelled back. "Did you want something?"

"It's Seth," Diana waved the phone.

Summer's mouth dropped open. Austin rolled his eyes. After a moment he climbed down off the roof, then helped Summer down. When he reached for her waist, she pushed his hands away irritably.

Diana sauntered down the walkway. She could see Summer working up an excuse, a logical explanation for why she happened to be playing tonsil hockey with someone other than her fiancé.

"Just a sec, Seth," Diana said. "Summer's a little busy."

There was a pause on the other end of the line. "Diana?" Seth said at last. "I never really got a chance to thank you for straightening me out over spring break. I was so angry about seeing Summer with Austin that I guess I couldn't see the forest for the trees, you know? You were right. I couldn't exactly get all irate when you and I had done the same . . . well, anyway, thanks."

"Sure," Diana said softly as she neared the stilt house. "Anytime. I'm a regular marriage counselor. Oh. I almost forgot." She paused in front of a stricken-looking Summer. "Congratulations on your engagement. I'm sure you two will be very happy."

With a knowing smile, Diana passed the phone to Summer. Austin's face was impassive, but Summer looked so terrified and confused that Diana almost felt sorry for her.

Almost.

Diana turned on her heel and headed back to the main house. Summer's too-animated voice chirped away like the birds in the trees.

All too vividly Diana could picture Seth out in California in his dark little apartment. Near his bed would be a picture of dear old Summer. He would kiss it at night, he would dream about her, he would fill his fantasies with her.

In the meantime, Summer was busy filling her fantasies with Austin.

Kind, sweet, good-hearted Seth. He deserved better than that.

He deserved someone like Diana.

Maybe it was time to give Mallory's assistant a call about that ticket to California.

After Seth hung up, Summer clutched the portable phone tightly, as if she were holding his hand. His last *I love you* rang in her ear like a shrill alarm.

Austin was leaning with his back to the railing. "I take it that was my competition?"

"Seth is not your competition. You have no competition."

Austin smiled.

"You know what I mean."

"You didn't mention me," Austin said accusingly.

"You didn't come up." Summer glanced

over her shoulder nervously. "I'm afraid Diana thinks we were . . . you know."

"But we weren't you-knowing. We had you-know interruptus." Austin raised his brows. "Although I got the feeling you would have you-knowed if you-know-who hadn't called."

Summer felt the guilt boiling up inside her. It was bad enough before, when she'd been attracted to Austin over spring break. But now she was an engaged woman, a woman with a great big symbol on her left hand (well, maybe not so big) that told the world she'd found Mr. Right.

Summer joined Austin at the railing. Vivid dawn colors spilled across the surface of the bay. A silver fish popped into the air like a wingless bird, then gently splash-landed.

"I'm going to tell you something, Austin," Summer said evenly. "Just so you understand." She cleared her throat.

"I'm all ears."

"After you left me, I told Seth the whole truth. About how I felt about you, I mean." She stole a glance at Austin. His hopeful gaze made her stiffen, but she pressed on. "I told him that if you had stayed, I wasn't sure what I would have done. I told him that . . . that I'd had real feelings for you."

"I knew you did," he said. The sound of

triumph in his voice told her he hadn't really been so sure.

"But then time went on, and you were gone, and I realized just how much I'd always loved Seth. I realized that I want to spend the rest of my life with him."

"You can't possibly know that," Austin scoffed.

"Why not?"

"Because for starters, it's crazy to talk about your whole life that way." Austin looked down into the placid water. "Who knows what your whole life even means? I don't presume I'll live till the ripe old age of ninety with my high school sweetheart. In my family, it just hasn't worked out that way for some of us. Our genes have other ideas."

For a moment Summer wondered if he was going to cry, but his mouth hardened into a tight line of resolve.

"And besides," Austin continued, "just because you have a high school diploma, Summer, doesn't mean you understand the workings of the universe. You haven't had enough experience to make a life-changing decision like getting engaged."

"Oh, and you have? How many girlfriends are enough to know, Austin? Three? A dozen? A hundred? What if girl number one hundred and three is the right one, and you settle for number one hundred and two?"

Austin looked at her and sighed. "All I know is that I am madly in love with you, right now, this instant. I don't know where either of us will be or how we'll feel next October, or five years from now. . . ." His voice trailed off. "Or for however long we're around. I can't make promises, Summer. Promises are like that glitter on your finger. They can get lost way too easily. Look at all the divorces in the world. You think those people didn't mean it when they said 'till death do us part'?"

Summer moved her left hand, watching her diamond flash softly. In her parents' wedding album there was a picture of her mother gazing fondly at her own diamond ring. It had caught the dazzling light of the photographer's flash, making it look far bigger than it really was.

"How can you settle for Seth when you haven't even given me a chance?" Austin asked.

"There's a difference between settling and making a choice, Austin. I've made my choice."

He shrugged. "Well, it's not like I'm going away. I don't give up easily, Summer. I almost lost you once already."

"I think you should probably go now."

"You can keep the muffins."

"Thanks."

"You still getting a place with Marquez and Diana?"

She nodded.

"Whereabouts?"

"We haven't decided."

"You wouldn't move without leaving a forwarding address, would you?"

She smiled a little. "You bet I would."

"I'll find you." Slowly Austin turned to leave, then hesitated. "I guess you're not up for a good-bye you-know?"

"How about a handshake?"

Austin took both her hands in his and held tight. He looked down at her ring. "Before long, that ring will be off your finger," he said confidently.

"It's never coming off," Summer replied.

She didn't sound nearly as confident.

9

Anchors Aweigh

"Five more minutes," Marquez vowed, waving to Diver as she ran by him on the beach. She was still feeling exhausted from her graduation party the night before, but exhaustion was no excuse not to exercise.

Diver was sitting on the white sand in his swim trunks, watching her with a look that said he just didn't get it. Well, Diver didn't have to get it. He was naturally lean and could eat whatever he wanted. Whereas Marquez could eat a potato chip and watch it instantly take up residence on her hips.

Marquez picked up her pace a little, although she was so winded she was sucking air like a vacuum hose. She nodded to a jogger passing her on the wet sand. She'd never had a clue how many people were up at the crack of dawn like this, dashing across the beach as though they had a bus to catch.

She'd flirted with exercise over the years, of course. Read the magazines that told her "Twenty Minutes a Day Is All It Will Take to a Shapelier You." Mostly she'd just rolled her eyes at all the people trying so hard to turn themselves into Cindy Crawford clones.

But now things were different. Marquez wasn't sure why. They just were.

Exercise was only the beginning. Marquez had bought one of those little food scales so that she could tell how many ounces of Grape-Nuts she really was consuming. She'd learned to cut up her food into tiny bits and savor it, morsel by morsel.

And it had paid off. She'd heard it in the compliments of friends and casual acquaintances. She'd felt it in the way what she called her "fat jeans" hung slackly from her newly thinner hips.

Of course, Diana said she was losing too fast. And Diver said it, too. But what did they know? They were congenitally, pathologically, unfairly thin people.

Diver, strangely, hadn't once said anything about her new and improved look, which just told Marquez the obvious: She was still way too fat. She couldn't exactly expect him to compliment her. A guy as gorgeous as Diver was practically accosted by beautiful girls everywhere he went.

Marquez gulped at the air, arms and legs pumping, sweat trickling down her chest. When she reached the little dock that signaled her turnaround point, she allowed herself to slow up just a little. Her thighs and calves were searing with pain, but that was the price she had to pay for all those surreptitious Milky Ways over the years.

She turned, veering past a giddy Labrador retriever out for a run with its female owner, and headed back to the spot where Diver sat anchored to the sand.

That's what he was, her anchor.

The word had come to her that morning, after loading the last chair into the cramped U-Haul and kissing her mother and father and brothers good-bye. Thank God for Diver. Thank God he's there for me right now. My parents are leaving, and my house is being taken over by strangers. I'm done with high school, and I'm not sure I can swing college. And my ex-boyfriend is out running around with a girl who looks like Kate Moss on Slim-Fast.

Diver is my anchor. That's what Marquez had told herself while tears had streamed down her face and she'd promised her mom and dad and brothers all kinds of things. I'll write every day, I'll take my vitamins, I'll get a nice job, I'll eat more, yes, I promise I'll eat more.

She'd watched the U-Haul grumble away down the tiny palm-lined street where she'd grown up. Then she'd climbed in her ancient Honda and hightailed it up the coast to Diver's place.

She was getting Jell-O legs, all wobbly and uncertain. The sand made running so hard, but that was good. Hard was good because hard meant more calories were being burned away. She hadn't eaten that morning, which was even better. That way the exercise wasn't wasted on her disgusting, never-ending appetite, the little weak beast inside of her.

Diver smiled as she neared. He was so intensely handsome. She knew that when people saw them together, they never dreamed she and Diver were boyfriend and girlfriend. They were so mismatched. It wasn't just because he was a golden boy from Swedish and English stock and she was Cuban-American. It was because he was a perfect, chiseled specimen of humanity and she was a shapeless blob of tan-colored Play-Doh. But that was going to change.

She loved Diver with all her heart. She was going to keep him, somehow. Somehow she would find a way to be sure he never left her, the way J.T. had left her.

Marquez dropped onto the sand beside

Diver. Her head was swimming as though she'd just spent an hour in the spin cycle of her parents' old Maytag. She put her head between her legs and tried to breathe.

"Hey," Diver said, rubbing her back, "you okay?"

"Fine. Just . . . winded."

"You sure?"

"I'm fine. It's the price we jocks pay." Marquez wiped the sweat off her brow and checked her watch. "Man, I should get going soon. Diana and Summer and I are going apartment hunting today." She dropped her head onto his hard, sun-warmed shoulder. "I wish you weren't so far away. This drive is murder. I don't suppose you'd like to be a fourth roommate?"

Diver laughed. "My sister wouldn't like that."

"She'd get over it." Marquez grinned. "And you could share a room with me. Think of the possibilities."

"I've thought of the possibilities," Diver said, kissing her softly. He had a way of brushing his lips over hers that sent ripples of longing down to her toes. It was as intense and fleeting as a flash of heat lightning.

Marquez wished Diver would say, "Yes, sure, I'll move in with you," but of course he wouldn't. Not with Summer there. And probably not even if

Marquez had a whole place to herself. Diver was a loner. He liked his privacy. He wasn't ready for a relationship like that yet. And maybe Marquez wasn't either. She sometimes spent the night at Diver's, but they never did anything, never crossed the line. Sure, they made out for long, passionate, wonderful hours. But that was as far as it ever went. It seemed to be the way Diver wanted it.

Marquez wasn't sure what she'd do if Diver were more like J.T. With J.T., it had always been like a game of keep-away, with Marquez dodging and scolding and finding a billion different ways to say, "No, I'm not ready for that, J.T."

But with Diver . . . she wasn't so sure. Maybe it would make them closer. Maybe then she would be sure she could hold on to him.

"There's something I've been wanting to tell you," Diver said, trailing a finger through the sand.

"How much you adore me?"

"You know I do." Diver smiled tolerantly. He always just assumed Marquez understood how he felt, as if she were a mind reader. He hoarded words like gold, doling them out with care. "There's a new wildlife rehabilitation center opening down on Coconut Key. They're looking for help, and I thought I might apply. . . ."

Marquez's heart jumped. "Diver, if Diana and Summer and I can find a place there, then you and I would be in the same town. That would be fantastic!"

He nodded. "It would be." He glanced over his shoulder at the makeshift tree house he'd been living in for the last few months. "I'd miss it here, but it would be good to be near you. And I can't stay here forever. This new job would mean more training." He made a face. "Summer said I can't hide out and escape forever. It made me . . . think. Don't tell her that, though."

Marquez squeezed his hand. "Apply, okay? I'd feel so much better if you were closer."

"Okay," Diver said. He kissed her again, and she shivered a little.

After a while she stood on reluctant legs. "Where are you going?" Diver asked.

"I got my wind back. I thought I'd do another lap."

He pulled on her arm. "Stay here," he said softly. "No more running for a while, okay? Let's just sit and watch the waves."

Marquez hesitated. "I'll be back before you know it," she promised. "The waves can wait." She took off down the sand before he could answer.

Two more laps, Marquez thought as she ran. She could pull off two.

Maybe even three, if she really tried. The waves could wait. And so could Diver.

10

In Search of the Perfect Apartment

> 11:35 A.M.: *Quaint 2 bedroom, 1 bath apartment. Tub with feet, fireplace, charm to spare. Must see to believe!*

"Well," Summer said, clearing her throat, "I see it, but I don't believe it."

"At least they weren't lying about the tub," Marquez said. "It has feet, all right."

Diana sighed. "So do the rats."

"We'll think about it," Summer told the manager.

> 12:15 P.M.: *Immaculate 1 BR den. No smokers. Won't last.*

"So, yes or no?" the caretaker asked. She took a long drag on her Marlboro.

"I was sort of wondering where the den was," Summer said. "We were going to use it as a second bedroom."

The woman pointed.

"But that's a closet," Marquez protested.

Another satisfied puff. "It's got a door on it, right?" the woman asked hoarsely.

Marquez nodded.

"It's got an outlet in it, right?"

"You mean, to plug stuff in?" Summer asked.

The woman rolled her eyes. "First apartment, huh?" She jangled her keys. "It's got an outlet, it's got a door, it's a den. Yes or no?"

"We'll think about it," Summer said.

1:20 P.M.: *Sunny bungalow, pets okay, eat-in kitchen, AC, steps to beach.*

"It's hot in here," Diana said.

"Sweltering," Marquez agreed. "I thought this place had air-conditioning."

Summer pointed to the ceiling fan.

"Oh," Marquez said wearily.

"Beach access, too." The manager jerked his thumb. "A mile and a quarter up the highway."

Summer checked the ad. "Just a few steps," she quoted.

"Yeah," Marquez muttered, "if you're the Jolly Green Giant."

"We'll think about it," Summer told the manager.

> 2:10 P.M.: *Beautiful, quiet, secure 2 BR, 2 bath. Walk to shops. Caring management.*

"It really *is* beautiful," Summer murmured as Diana parked her car.

"And quiet and secure. And you really could walk to downtown," Marquez added excitedly.

A balding middle-aged man appeared from behind the building. Gold chains sparkled around his neck. His huge stomach strained at the buttons of his sweat-stained shirt.

He gave an enthusiastic wave. "Well, well, it's my lucky day," he called. "You the gals who called about the apartment?"

"I'm guessing that would be the caring management," Diana said with a sigh.

"We'll think about it," Summer called.

Diana floored the gas pedal.

"The thing is, I'm about to be homeless." Marquez sipped at her diet Coke that afternoon. The girls sat at a wobbly table, the rental ads spread between them.

The air in the little café was sultry. The restaurant was on the bottom floor of a yellow house located on a tiny cobblestoned street filled with shops and restaurants that backed onto the water.

"You're not homeless. You can always stay with Diana or me till we find a place," Summer assured her.

"The new people are moving in next Monday," Marquez said sullenly. "I have to have all my stuff out by then."

Diana folded the paper and pushed a damp lock of hair off her forehead. "Man, it's hot. We could have at least picked a restaurant with air-conditioning."

"I think it's charming," Summer said, "in a tacky sort of way. There's a bookstore attached to the café and everything."

"I do like Coconut Key a lot," Marquez said. "There's more to do than there was on Crab Claw. There are restaurants and a movie theater and a mall. And it's a college town. FCU's here, so Diana and I would be all set this fall—assuming, that is, I can get together enough cash to cover books and stuff. And there'd be a lot more people our age than on Crab Claw." She grinned. "More male meat on parade."

"Summer doesn't need more male meat," Diana said dryly. "She's getting plenty. If anything, Summer needs to go on a vegetarian kick for a while."

Marquez looked at Diana curiously, then at Summer. "What's she talking about?"

Summer shrugged uncomfortably. She really didn't want to get into it.

"Summer had a little visitor this morning," Diana said, smirking. "Or I guess I should say a big visitor. How tall is Austin, Summer? About six-two?"

"Austin came to see you?" Marquez cried.

"He lives around here now," Summer said flatly.

"You *are* kidding." Marquez peered at Summer. "Whoa, wait a minute. You are *not* kidding?"

"What are the odds?" Diana said, leaning back in her chair with a cool smile.

"He just said hello," Summer said. "He brought me some muffins."

"Hmm . . . is that what they call it in Minnesota?" Diana inquired. She leaned toward Marquez. "He brought her muffins in a major way, if you get my drift."

"Diana!" Summer nearly shouted. "We were not kissing, if that's what you're thinking. We were . . . thinking about kissing, I admit, but that's all. At the last minute we didn't. And even if we had kissed—which we didn't—it would have been just for old times' sake."

She finished her speech just as the waitress approached. She was a pretty black girl about their age, wearing the worn expression of someone near the end of her shift. She placed plates of hamburgers and fries in front of Diana and Summer.

"You sure you don't want anything?" she asked Marquez.

"I'm fine," Marquez said.

"I've got plenty of cash, Marquez," Diana offered, "if—"

"I'm not destitute, I'm just not hungry, Mom."

"Okay, then. You need anything else here?" the girl asked.

"Yeah," Marquez muttered. "An apartment would be nice."

The girl shook her head. "It's tough finding anything on Coconut. You've got students and retirees and snowbirds all fighting for the same real estate." She snapped her fingers. "You know, though, there might be a place . . . but no, it's kind of weird. You're looking for a three-bedroom?"

"We're looking for anything with a roof and a toilet," Summer said.

"I'd settle for a Porta Potti," Marquez said.

"You mind if I sit?" The girl straddled a chair. "Sorry, I'm breaking in new Docs. I'm Blythe, by the way."

"That's Diana," Summer said, "that's Marquez, and I'm Summer."

"Cool name." Blythe smiled. "The thing is—" She lowered her voice. "There's a place here. On the top floor. I probably shouldn't say anything, 'cause it might be taken, but it's sort of cool, in a weird way. It's this converted attic, so all the walls are slanted, and I think maybe there are only two bedrooms. There's a little pool out back, and you can see the ocean, which is great. The landlady—my boss—is completely wacky, but it's a great location and dirt cheap. I live on the second floor."

"You think we could take a look at it?" Summer asked hopefully.

"See, there's this new guy working here—he is so gorgeous, incidentally, and the girls are falling all over themselves. But anyway, he might be taking it. I don't know. I haven't worked with him in a few shifts. Could be he found another place."

"This would be so perfect," Marquez cried. "We'd be right in the center of town, and the ocean's right there, and I'd be close to Di—" She snapped her jaw closed.

"Close to what?" Summer asked.

"Or should we say *whom?*" Diana asked.

"*Who,*" Marquez corrected.

"No, *whom,*" Diana said.

"I'm pretty sure it's *who*—"

"Who, what, which, whatever, just tell us what the deal is!" Diana snapped.

Marquez rolled her eyes. "I didn't say anything because I knew it would freak Summer out." She paused. "The thing is, Diver might be moving down here. There's a wildlife place, like the one he works at, opening up, and he's going to apply. So it's not definite or anything. Besides, he's going to be around, Summer, one way or another."

"I know," Summer said, tearing at her napkin. "It's okay, Marquez. I have no right to interfere in your love life."

"Well," Blythe interrupted, looking a little uncomfortable, "I've got ketchup bottles to fill."

"Sorry," Marquez apologized. "We got sidetracked there on personal stuff."

"I know how that goes." Blythe stood and pushed in her chair. "Tell you what. I'll ask my boss about the place. If Austin doesn't want it, maybe you can go on up and take a peek. It's probably a mess—"

"Austin." Summer said it in a very low voice.

"Yeah, he's the new guy."

"Tall, dark, looks like trouble?" Diana asked.

Blythe grinned. "That's the one."

Summer pushed back her plate. "We are outta here."

"Wait a minute, Summer," Marquez pleaded, grabbing her arm. "Can't we at least take a look at it?"

"I am not living where Austin works," Summer declared. "No way."

"I take it you know Austin?" Blythe asked.

"Oh, she knows him, all right," Diana said.

"Oh. Like, *knows* him."

"Only I'm trying very hard not to know him anymore," Summer said sternly. "I'm sorry, Marquez, but we'll just have to keep looking."

"We've *been* looking." Marquez crossed her arms over her chest. "I don't see why your personal life is the only deciding factor here. I am practically broke and soon to be homeless. I need a job and I need a place, and I need them fast. And between avoiding Austin and Diver, you're going to end up making us live in Maine or something."

Summer looked at Marquez with concern. Her hand was shaking just a little, and she looked near tears. It wasn't like Marquez to get so worked up. Usually she'd just laugh it off and tell Summer to lighten up.

"You know," Blythe said, "if you need a job, there's always something here. The tips are nothing special, but you can scarf all the food you want."

"I could have a job *and* an apartment, maybe," Marquez said, glaring at Summer and managing to make her feel completely crummy.

"Marquez has a point," Diana said. "I mean, if you and Austin are just friends, Summer, what's there to worry about?"

Summer caught the gleam in her cousin's eye. She knew what Diana was implying. If

Summer was really committed to Seth, what was the problem?

Marquez was looking at her with hope, Diana with challenge. Fine, then. She could handle it. She could handle Austin Shaw just fine.

"Ask your manager if the apartment's available, would you, Blythe?" Summer said at last.

"And if it is?" Marquez challenged.

Summer took a deep breath. "And if it is," she replied, "we'll think about it."

11

Constellations and Other Very Important Stuff

"Seth? Hi, it's me." Summer lay on her bed in the stilt house. Through the open kitchen window she could see the night sky, heavy with stars. The wind was up, and the waves grumbled loudly as they hit the shore. "I'm in the stilt house."

"Is anything wrong?"

Summer could hear the concern in Seth's voice. She tried to imagine him in his new apartment in California, the one he shared with other guys from the boat building company. But she couldn't even seem to conjure up a decent image of his face.

"Nothing's wrong, no." She reached for the photo on her nightstand of Seth and her at the prom. They'd posed for the photo shortly after

Seth had proposed. They looked breathless and dizzy, as though they'd just climbed off the world's fastest roller coaster.

"How's the apartment hunting going?"

Summer set the picture aside. "Um, we found one, maybe. It's on Coconut Key, and Marquez and Diana really love it. But I'm not so sure."

Seth laughed. "Like you three will ever agree on anything. Why don't you like it?"

"Well, it's on the top floor of this house, an attic, really. So the walls are all slanted."

"And?"

"And that's it. Who wants to live in a place where you have to walk tilted all the time?"

"Well, I guess I can see your point. This place I'm sharing isn't exactly a palace. It's right near my job, which is cool, but sharing an apartment with three other slobby guys isn't paradise. I wish it were you instead."

"I miss you."

"I miss you more. How's your ring holding up?"

Summer held out her hand. The diamond winked at her in reproach. "So far, so good. I almost took it off to do the dishes today, but I was afraid I'd lose it."

"Don't lose it, whatever you do. It wiped out my savings."

"I love you, Seth."

"I love you, too."

"I should hang up. It's late."

"Okay. I'll call you next."

"You hang up first," Summer said.

"No, you."

"I love you," Summer said. She started to disconnect, then hesitated. "You still there?"

"Yeah."

"Okay, this time I'm really hanging up." She heard Seth saying "I love you" again as she clicked off the phone.

Summer closed her eyes, listening to the relentless waves. What's wrong with the apartment? Well, I'll tell you, Seth. It's just a few steps away from Austin, and something tells me that's not exactly the ideal location.

After a few moments Summer reached for the phone and punched in her phone number in Bloomington. Was it really her number anymore? Where was home now? The stilt house? The University of Wisconsin, where she and Seth would be going to school that fall? Some slant-walled attic apartment on Coconut Key?

When she heard her mother's voice, Summer's eyes pooled with tears. "Mom? Did I wake you?"

"No, I was just putzing around, waiting for Leno to come on. You okay, honey?"

"I'm okay. I just . . . I miss you, is all."

"Oh, I miss you, too, hon. This house is just

so empty now, with Diver and you . . . and your dad . . . gone. I feel sort of abandoned."

"Are you holding up all right?"

"Oh, you know. Good days, bad days. Hey, guess what I did today? I got an application to U of M. I'm thinking of going back to school, maybe getting my master's in social work. What do you think?"

"I think that's fantastic, Mom."

"Me, too. Although it scares the hell out of me. Wouldn't that be so nineties—mother and daughter in college at the same time?" She laughed a little too hard.

"I wish I were home. I'd take you out to celebrate."

"Well, I'll see you plenty this fall. UW's just a quick drive. I'll force you to come visit me in my dorm room."

"You're not really getting a dorm room?"

"No, no." A pause. "But the thing is, honey . . . Dad and I are going to go ahead with the divorce for sure. And when everything's finalized, well, we both agree there's no point in keeping this big old house."

Summer took a shuddery breath. "You're going to sell the house?"

"We have to, Summer. It just wouldn't make sense to keep it. Maybe I'll get one of those condos in Edina—you know, the fake gingerbready ones out by the mall?"

"Those are cute," Summer said without feeling.

"Don't be sad, honey."

"I'm not. I mean, I am. But I'm sadder for you."

"Don't be. I'm a tough old broad."

"You're not so old," Summer said. She gazed out the window. The stars were cluttered in the sky like tossed silver coins. She wondered how astronomers made sense out of them all. Seth knew lots of constellations—Orion and Aquarius and Pegasus, all those.

"Mom?"

"Hmm?"

"Did you ever think, when you married Dad, that it would turn out this way? Did you have any doubts that maybe he wasn't the right one, maybe there was someone else even more . . . right?"

Her mother laughed. "Oh, I suppose so. I think everybody does. Everybody who's honest with herself." She hesitated. "Your dad and I were so young when we got married. How can you make a decision at the age of nineteen that's supposed to last the rest of your life?" She paused again. "It's something you should think about, too, sweetheart."

Summer took a deep breath. "I know," she said. "I will."

After she hung up, Summer closed her eyes

and hugged her pillow and tried to picture Seth. But to her frustration, Austin kept making unannounced appearances. Finally she turned her attention to the stars hugging the horizon. She thought maybe she saw Orion, but it was hard to tell.

She'd have to ask Seth. He would know for sure.

"Just one more thing," Marquez promised.

Diver looked at her incredulously. He'd been packing her Honda all morning, despite heat in the low nineties. His shoulders and chest shone with sweat. His face was flushed. He looked as frustrated as Diver ever really looked—mellow, by most people's standards, but Marquez knew better.

"I can't leave Geraldo behind."

"Geraldo," Diver repeated. "The mangy, smelly, stained stuffed elephant you keep on your bed?"

"That mangy elephant knows all my deepest, darkest secrets."

Diver smiled grudgingly. "Well, then, bring the dude along. So what if I have to ride on the roof?"

"He'll fit. He's mushy."

"Where will he fit, exactly?"

He pointed to the car in the driveway of Marquez's soon-to-be-former house. The entire backseat and trunk overflowed with art supplies, half-dead plants, clothes in Hefty bags, framed paintings from Marquez's art classes, photo albums, a handful of mismatched pots and pans Marquez's mother had left for her, sheets and pillows, and a huge cardboard box marked Very Important Stuff.

"There's room on the passenger side," Marquez said. "Geraldo can ride on your lap."

Diver wiped his brow with the back of his arm. "It's a good thing that I love you."

When they were finally done lugging things out to the car, Marquez stood in her vast, empty bedroom, which had been a ground-floor ice cream parlor once upon a time. The hardwood floor was spattered with color, a Crayola-box palette of drizzles and splashes. But it was on the walls that Marquez had truly left her mark. Giant murals extended from floor to ceiling, the once bare brick covered with dazzling scenes. Palm trees and birds, sunsets and sunrises, anything and everything that she'd felt like painting over the years. There were names, too, a graffitilike maze of friends and teachers, movie star crushes and boys of the month.

"Jared Leto, huh?" Diver murmured, his arm draped around Marquez's shoulder as they studied a wall.

"Just a passing phase."

Marquez caught a glimpse of herself in the

full-length mirror on the back of her closet door. She was wearing a pair of old shorts she'd almost given up on. Now they hung loosely on her. Still, her butt looked disgustingly huge. She tugged down her baggy T-shirt, hoping to disguise the awful truth.

"What was there?" Diver pointed to the thick layer of black paint in the corner, where bits and pieces of red letters still poked through.

Marquez shrugged. "J.T. He got spray-painted out of existence."

"I wish it were that easy," Diver said softly.

Marquez looked at him. "What do you mean?"

"Nothing. Just that it takes time, that's all." He moved close to the wall, running his fingers over the glossy layers of paint. "Where am I?"

"There, next to Summer's name."

"Linked by blood and paint."

"Let's go," Marquez muttered. Suddenly she couldn't stand it anymore. She could imagine the new people coming in, bitching about the way she'd ruined the room, painting over the walls in some sunny pastel. Well, it would take about a hundred layers of off-white latex to cover *those* walls. She could take some satisfaction in that, at least.

They left the house quietly. Marquez locked the door behind her. "You'll have new walls soon," Diver assured her.

"Not like those." Marquez climbed into the front seat of her Honda. The sun-heated vinyl seat burned her thighs.

"Well, at least you managed to talk Summer into taking the apartment," Diver said as he climbed in beside her, Geraldo clutched in his arms.

"After two more wasted days of searching," Marquez said with a grin. "That girl can be stubborn. But she caved in the end."

Diver nodded thoughtfully. "She can be tough to get through to."

"Family trait," Marquez said affectionately, patting Diver's knee. "It's in your blood."

"Maybe. I don't know, though. My dad . . . my other dad . . . he was stubborn, too."

"You mean the one who took you?"

Diver nodded.

"How about his wife?"

There was no answer. Diver was busy trying to reattach Geraldo's right eye.

"Diver?" Marquez said gently. "If you ever wanted to talk about them, you could. You know that, right?"

"I know. But that's over. I want it to go away."

Marquez started the car. She wasn't going to push it. She and Diver were alike that way. They didn't like to dissect things and dwell on them, the way Summer and Diana did. When

Marquez felt bad, she liked to drive or dance or paint. A couple of times, when she'd felt really low, she'd even tried drinking. But that had left her with worse feelings and horrible hangovers. So now she stuck to her art, mostly.

Diver, when he felt bad, just stared at the ocean and climbed inside himself. It made Marquez feel a little lonely when that happened, but she understood why he did it, and she didn't push.

"Well, good-bye, house," she said softly, backing out of the drive. She wiped away a tear, feeling annoyed. It was just a house, not a shrine.

She drove down the narrow streets of the key, passing familiar landmarks along the way. The spot where her brother Miguel had broken his wrist skateboarding. The corner of Palm and Lido, where she'd kissed her sixth-grade crush on a dare. The Crab 'n' Conch, where the food was lousy and the service wasn't a whole lot better.

"I think I may have a job," Marquez said as she braked at the four-way stop in the center of town. Two guys shouldering a red surfboard sauntered past. "Waiting tables at this café place on the ground floor of our apartment building. The landlady owns it. She says I can pick up shifts, see how I do."

"Great," Diver said. "If I get that job at the

wildlife rehab center, we'll both be gainfully employed."

They'd just started across the intersection when she heard someone yell. Marquez knew it was J.T. even before she turned to see him. His new girlfriend, the one Marquez had discovered him in bed with, hung off his arm. She was giggling loudly.

J.T. waved. "Hey, Marquez, where you goin' with Geraldo?"

Marquez hit the gas, ignoring him.

After a few blocks, Diver asked, "You all right?"

"I'm fine," she said. Her body felt tight with compressed energy. Maybe she'd go for a run later, a long one.

"It'll get easier."

"Look, it's over with me and J.T., okay? I don't really want to talk about it."

Diver played with Geraldo's eye. "Okay. I know how that goes."

Marquez cranked up the radio. Green Day, nice and loud. She drove as fast as she figured she could get away with. The backseat was piled so high with stuff that she couldn't see out the rearview mirror, but that was okay by her.

She wasn't planning on looking back, anyway.

12

Diamonds Are Not Always a Girl's Best Friend

"You know, I'm starting to sense what this apartment needs," Diana said as she dug a camera out of a cardboard box. "I think it's called furniture."

"We have a mildewy couch left by the previous tenants," Summer pointed out. "Plus a mildewy chair and a mildewy table. And the landlady said she's got plenty of mildewy mattresses in the storage shed."

Diana aimed the camera at Summer. "You're right. It's not like we don't have a decorating motif. Mildew goes with everything. By the way, smile. I'm breaking in my new camera and recording our move-in for posterity."

Summer stuck out her tongue, and Diana clicked the camera.

Marquez and Diana had been right about one thing, Summer thought: It *was* a quaint apartment. Despite the sloping roof, the place was surprisingly big. It featured one large bedroom flanked by a bathroom, with a smaller bedroom on the other side. The kitchen, which was really just an extension of the living room, was even more dated than the one in the stilt house. But the polished pine floors gleamed, and the arched windows let in plenty of light, even affording a view of the ocean.

If it weren't for the little Austin problem, it would have been just about perfect.

"Knock, knock, male coming, everyone decent?" Marquez called from the stairway.

Summer busied herself dragging a suitcase into one of the bedrooms. She wished Marquez could have at least let them get settled in before bringing Diver over. But sooner or later, Summer knew, she was going to have to get used to seeing him.

She took a deep breath and headed back into the living room. Diver was holding a box of silverware and a big stuffed elephant. He met Summer's eyes reluctantly.

"Smile," Diana commanded, turning her camera on Diver, but he didn't react.

"Look, you two," Marquez said, marching across the room with two plastic bags of clothes in tow, "I love you both, and you're just going to have to get used to being in the same room together. I'm tired of tiptoeing around your feelings. Summer, say hi to your brother."

Summer toyed with her diamond ring, avoiding Diver's gaze. "Hi."

"Diver, say hi to your sister."

"Hi," he said softly.

"There." Marquez dropped the bags. "Now, was that so difficult?" She wrinkled her nose. "What is that smell?"

"It's our decorating theme," Diana said. "Early American mildew."

"Man, let's open some windows, already."

"They *are* open."

"Doors, then." Marquez swung open the louvered French doors that opened onto a wide balcony. "Look at this view," she said. "This is so fantastic."

Summer, Diana, and Diver joined her on the balcony. An ornate wrought-iron fence wrapped around the veranda. Trumpet vines, thick with bright orange flowers, wove in and out of the railing. An ancient oak tree shaded the porch, its limbs heavy with Spanish moss. The entire street below was lined with little shops and restaurants in turn-of-the-century buildings.

"How could you not have wanted to live here?" Marquez asked Summer. "What a great location. And my new job is right downstairs." She sighed. "Of course, it's not exactly like my old house."

Summer patted her back. "I bet it was hard to leave your murals, huh?"

Marquez shrugged. "I'll do a new one here. Maybe something on the ceiling. Sort of our own little Sistine Chapel."

"Whoa," Diana said, making a time-out sign. "Before you start redecorating, let's try to do something tasteful. Like, say, putting that elephant out of his misery."

"Like your coffin's going to blend in, Diana."

Diana rolled her eyes. "I'm going to measure the living room," she said. "Maybe we can steal one of Mallory's leather couches."

"I think we should do this on our own," Summer said to Marquez. "Start from scratch."

Marquez elbowed her. "Did you smell that couch?"

"But if we let Diana borrow from home, it'll be like it's her place, not ours."

"You're right," Marquez conceded. "And I'm already feeling kind of placeless at the moment."

"Me, too. I talked to my mom last night, and she said—" Suddenly Summer realized Diver was listening intently.

"Said what?"

"Nothing. Just . . . well, she and my dad are

selling the house." She shot a look at Diver, but he'd turned away. He was staring impassively at a bee drowsing near one of the trumpet flowers.

Just then there was a knock at the door. "Anybody home?" a voice called from the stairwell.

"We have company, girls," Diana announced.

Blythe was standing in the doorway, a plate of muffins in her hand. Someone was standing behind her. A guy.

With a sudden flash of horror, Summer realized it was Austin. Like Blythe, he was wearing a black T-shirt with Jitters, the café's name, on the pocket. He was carrying something small and square wrapped in tissue paper.

"Well, well, the plot thickens," Diana said, grinning slyly at Summer. "Come on in."

"We brought you welcome-to-the-neighborhood muffins," Blythe said. "Left over from this morning, but hey, they're still good."

"Great! I'm starving," Diana said, grabbing one.

"None for me, thanks," Marquez said.

"Me either," Summer said, glaring at Austin.

"Told you she wasn't the muffin type," Austin whispered loudly to Blythe.

"Sit, everybody," Diana said. "You have your choice of mildewed couch or cardboard box. By the way, Blythe, this is Summer's brother and Marquez's boyfriend, Diver."

Blythe grinned at Diver. "Nice to meet you.

Sorry, I can't stay. I'm technically on duty, even though the café is totally dead."

"I can stay," Austin volunteered, dropping onto the couch. "I'm technically off duty."

"Thanks for stopping by, Blythe," Marquez said.

"Come by later," Summer added. "We might even have chairs and stuff." She turned to Austin. "We're a little busy here, Austin."

"Aren't you even going to open my house-warming gift?"

"No."

"Yes, we are," Diana said. She grabbed the present from Austin. "It's our first, if you don't count the muffins."

"It's really for Summer," Austin said, but Diana was already unwrapping the tissue paper. She held up a small frame. There were typed words inside.

"It's poetry," Austin volunteered. "e.e. cummings."

Marquez checked it out. "Nice," she commented. "I don't get it exactly, but I like the frame." She passed it over to Summer.

"Go ahead," Austin said. "Read it."

Reluctantly Summer scanned the words:

yes is a world
& in this world of
yes live

(skilfully curled)
all worlds
—e.e. cummings
"love is a place"
No Thanks (1935)

"It's very nice," she said politely.

Austin stretched out on the smelly couch. "Isn't it amazing how he could compress so much into those five lines?"

"But I don't get it," Marquez said. "What is she supposed to say yes to?"

"Take a guess," Diana said with a smirk.

Diver examined the poem. "No, it's not like that," he said after a moment. "It's more like saying yes to life, to . . . possibilities."

Austin nodded. "You ought to come to one of our poetry slams at the café sometime."

"Now *there's* a hot evening," Diana said. "Sign me up for sure."

Summer grabbed a cardboard box and began unpacking dishes wrapped in newspaper. "We really need to get to work, Austin."

"You're absolutely right." Austin sat up and clapped his hands. "Let's get down to business. Nice place, by the way. I almost took it, but it was too rich for my budget, and I don't need this much room. I live just a couple of blocks over."

"Oh, happy, happy, joy, joy," Diana said.

"So where do you want me?"

"Toledo would be nice," Summer muttered.

Austin laughed. "Alice, the landlady, told me you were thinking about painting the walls. She's got paint and brushes and stuff stashed in the storage room downstairs. Want me to see what's available?"

"Yes," Marquez said.

"No," Summer said.

"What color?" Diana asked.

"I'll take that as a maybe," Austin said cheerfully. With a wink at Summer, he headed for the stairs. "Back in a minute."

Summer pointed an accusing finger at Marquez when he was gone. "Why did you tell him yes to the paint?"

Marquez shrugged helplessly. "I don't know. Maybe it was that poem. It just popped out."

"I *told* you guys this would happen," Summer grumbled.

Diana began arranging silverware in a drawer. "Relax, Summer. Nothing is going to happen unless you want it to." She sent her a knowing look. "That is, as long as you remember how to say no."

"Remind me never to move again," Diana groaned a few hours later. She stretched out on the bedroom floor, her legs propped up against the low, slanting ceiling. Marquez lay beside her, her head in Diver's lap. In the next room, Austin and Summer were laughing loudly at some private joke.

"Have some more pizza, Marquez." Diana pushed the box across the floor. "All you ate was, like, a black olive."

"I'm too bushed to eat," Marquez said. She checked her watch. "That's got to be a world record. We painted the living room walls and unpacked three people's stuff, and it's only five-thirty." She poked at Diana's head with her toes. "You sure you're okay with the room division? It's not really fair, me getting one all to myself."

"Sure it is. First of all, you're the one who'll be generating all the paint fumes. And besides, you'll have Diver visiting, probably. At least until he gets that job."

"*If* I get that job," Diver amended.

Summer's musical giggle floated through the open doorway. "For someone who didn't want Austin around, she sure is enjoying having him here," Diana muttered. "How long does it take them to paint four walls, anyway?"

"I really think Summer just wants Austin to be a friend," Marquez said.

"You didn't see what I saw on the roof of the stilt house," Diana said.

"I don't get why you care, anyway." Marquez yawned. "I mean, it's Summer's love life, not yours."

Diana sat up. She was grouchy and antsy, and she felt like causing some trouble. "I just worry about Seth, is all. I really like him. He's a nice guy, and he deserves better than—" Austin laughed loudly, interrupting her. "He just plain deserves better."

Marquez sat up, too. Her dark eyes were narrowed suspiciously. "Since when do you care so much about Summer and Seth's relationship?"

"I'm their friend."

"So am I, but I didn't arrange for them to have a romantic spring break getaway on a private yacht. You did." She crossed her arms over her chest.

"Mallory knew the owner. Big deal. I invited you, too." Diana grinned. "And you know I don't care about you, Marquez."

"Still, it seems a little weird—"

Summer's frantic scream interrupted Marquez. "No! Oh, my God, where *is* it?"

Seconds later Summer rushed into the room. Her face and hands were smeared with white paint. "My ring! I can't find my ring!" She put her hands to her head, leaving a smudge of paint on her hair. "Help me, you guys!"

They followed her to the other room. Austin was scanning the floor. If he was smiling, it was hard to tell.

"Oh, no, oh, no, this is some kind of omen, isn't it?" Summer wailed. "Seth is going to kill me. He is going to totally kill me." She paced frantically back and forth, nearly knocking Austin over. "No, he's not going to kill me. I'll kill myself. It'll be less painful that way."

"Faster, too," Austin added.

"Would you please stop ranting long enough to tell us what happened?" Diana said.

"I . . . oh, God, I can't believe I was so *stupid!* . . . I took off my ring because I couldn't find any gloves and I didn't want to get paint on it." Summer peered under a sheet of newspaper. "So I took it off and put it on the windowsill in this Dixie cup."

"You put it on the windowsill?" Diana asked. "Wasn't that kind of asking for trouble?"

"Oh, fine, Diana, like I don't feel bad enough," Summer wailed.

"Sorry," Diana apologized. "But think how Seth is going to feel."

"I *am* thinking about how Seth is going to feel. First he'll feel terrible. Then he'll feel homicidal."

"Could be the other way around," Austin pointed out. "They say depression is anger turned inward—"

"Shut up, Austin!" Summer snapped. "You're the one who said it would be safe there. This is partly your fault."

"I don't see how I—"

"B-Because," Summer sobbed, "because the

other day you said I wouldn't be wearing my ring before long, and you were right. You . . . you were . . . psychotic. No—"

"Prescient?" Austin offered.

"Psychic?" Marquez tried.

"I don't know. One of those *p* words." Summer sniffled. "Oh, it's not your fault," she admitted, "it's mine."

"So losing it was kind of a Freudian slip, you mean?" Austin asked.

"Please shut up," Summer sobbed.

"Really, Austin, you're not helping matters," Marquez said. She put her hands on Summer's shoulders. "Get a grip, okay? This doesn't *mean* anything. It just happened. Now, let's get organized. When's the last time you saw the ring?"

"A few minutes ago. We were talking about whether to paint the ceiling, and Austin and I were fighting over who got the ladder. Then I noticed the Dixie cup on its side."

Marquez put her head out the window. "The roof is almost level, just a little bit slanted. Maybe the ring fell onto the ground."

"I'll go look," Diver offered.

"Me, too," Marquez said. "Summer, you and Austin and Diana scour the bedroom. Check the rest of the apartment, too. Maybe it just rolled somewhere."

"You know, you could probably pick up a

couple of extra shifts at the café and buy a new one," Austin said, grinning.

Summer groaned. "Maybe it wasn't the biggest ring, but it meant the world to me."

"That's obvious," Diana said sarcastically.

"What's that supposed to mean?" Summer demanded.

"Nothing," Diana said. "Let's everybody calm down and start looking. I'll check outside with Marquez and Diver. You two do the bedroom."

"We've already looked," Summer moaned. "It's totally hopeless."

Diana headed out the door. "Depends on how you look at things, I suppose," she said softly.

13

Marquez Can't Wait, but Austin Can

"Smile," Diana instructed, pointing her camera toward Marquez.

"I will not smile," Marquez said, panting. "I am sitting on an exercise bike, sweating like a giant porker. I am not in the mood to smile."

The sun had set, and the search for Summer's ring had long since been abandoned. Austin had talked Summer into going for a walk around town. Diana, Marquez, and Diver had stayed behind in the apartment. Diver was stacking cardboard boxes while Diana played with her camera and Marquez exercised.

"I'm warning you, Diana," Marquez barked. "Don't do it."

To Marquez's great annoyance, Diana snapped a picture anyway.

"How long are you going to ride?" Diana asked. "It's been, like, an hour."

"Come on, Marquez," Diver agreed as he broke down an empty box. "Hang out with us. It's been a long day."

"Another half-mile," Marquez muttered, feeling annoyed. It was going to take some time to get used to sharing her space this way. At home she'd had the entire downstairs to herself. She'd been able to paint or daydream or exercise to her heart's content. Without interference. Without commentary from some unfairly skinny audience.

Diana went to the kitchen window overlooking the backyard. "Summer and Austin are back," she reported. "They're heading for the pool patio. That was quite a long walk they took. Of course, she probably had to get over the terrible trauma of losing her ring."

"What is it with you and Summer and Austin?" Marquez asked breathlessly.

"Nothing. I just think after she made such an issue about not wanting to move here because of Austin, it's kind of strange that she's spent most of the day with him."

"I think you should leave that up to Summer," Diver said.

Diana held up her hands. "I'm just engaging in some idle speculation. Summer says she wants nothing to do with Austin, then she spends the day with him, loses her engagement ring, and spends more time with him. I think it's a little weird, is all."

Marquez stopped peddling. Sweat trickled down her forehead. Her feet felt glued to the pedals. She climbed off stiffly, like an old woman. The room spun for a moment. She grabbed the handlebars for support.

"You okay over there?" Diver asked.

Marquez nodded. "I'm feeling the burn."

"You're not supposed to exercise to the point of collapse, Marquez," Diana chided.

"Like you would know?"

"I read *Glamour*. I read *Sassy*. I know these things."

"Yeah, well, I read the numbers on my bathroom scale."

Diana shook her head. "Hey, they're your muscles. I just happen to prefer less-strenuous exercise."

"Like aerobic check-writing."

Diver pointed to the couch. "Why don't you sit down and recover?"

"Can't. I'm all sweaty. I need to take a shower."

"The first shower in our new apartment," Diana exclaimed.

"You are *not* photographing it for posterity, either," Marquez said.

"I wouldn't mind a copy of that picture," Diver said.

Diana trained her camera out the window. "You think Summer's going to tell Seth the truth about the ring?" She paused. "Or about Austin?"

Marquez hobbled toward the bathroom. She felt disoriented, the conversation buzzing past her like a tennis match she couldn't follow. "What?" she asked.

"Summer. You think she'll tell Seth?"

Marquez blinked. "Anybody seen my backpack?"

"Over by the door," Diver said. "Marquez? You sure you're okay? You look kind of pale."

"I just need a shower." Marquez grabbed her backpack. "See you in a minute. And no unauthorized photos, Diana."

"Yeah." Diana laughed. "The tabloids would pay big money to see you in the buff, Marquez."

Marquez closed the bathroom door behind her. Diana's comment stung. It was just a joke, just Diana mouthing off as usual, the kind of teasing Marquez had done herself a million times. So why were tears burning her eyes?

She wasn't tracking, wasn't making sense. She was so, so tired.

She needed to clear her head. A hot shower would be good. A hot shower, and then, maybe, the pills.

She locked the door and dug through her backpack for the little bottle.

She poured some into her palm. Little white pills. Her hands were shaking.

How many should she take? She should have asked.

She wanted to make them last. But when she ran out, she could always go back to the Cramp 'n' Croak. Willi, the day cook there, could always get her more, or if not Willi, plenty of other people she knew.

She put one on her tongue. Leaning her head into the old-fashioned porcelain sink, she turned on the tap and swallowed the pill.

That would be good for starters.

Marquez took off her clothes and stepped into the claw-footed tub. She pulled the curtain around her and turned the water on as hot as she could stand. The fine spray was like needles on her skin. The heat made her dizzy.

After a while she dried off and put on her terry robe. Already she felt a little buzzy. She wasn't sure what to expect. But she knew what she wanted.

She wanted the hunger to go away. She wanted to stop being so very, very tired.

She wanted to be thinner. Just a little thinner. And she didn't know why, but she just couldn't wait any longer. She had to make the need go away.

Her hair still dripping, she went into the living room and cuddled up next to Diver. Diana was out on the back balcony, camera in hand.

"You look better already," Diver said. He kissed her tenderly.

"Amazing what a shower can do for your outlook," Marquez said.

"Feeling any better?" Austin asked Summer.

"A little." Summer managed a halfhearted smile.

They were sitting in white chaises by the side of the little kidney-shaped pool behind the apartment. Thick palms filtered the rosy twilight rays. A tiny stone fountain featuring a decrepit-looking cherub trickled softly. The scent of jasmine was heavy in the air.

"I'm glad I wasn't working tonight and could be with you in your hour of need," Austin said.

Summer punched him in the arm. "I've had about enough of your sarcastic ring remarks."

"Hey, I'm the one who risked life and limb climbing out onto the roof to check the gutter. You know how old that roof is?"

"How old?"

"Real damn old, that's how old."

"Well, thanks. I'm glad you could stick around, too. For some reason, Diana seemed kind of mad at me about the whole thing. And Marquez has been really distracted lately. So I guess it was nice to have some moral support." She dipped her toe into the warm pool water. "Even if it was you."

"So you're sorry you told me to get lost when I showed up today?"

"I didn't exactly tell you to get lost."

"I recall some mention of Toledo."

Summer turned to face Austin. She thought for a moment. "Look, I won't deny I don't . . . mind having you around, Austin. And since it looks like there's no way to avoid it, with you working downstairs, all I ask is that we keep it just friends. Platonic. No complications. I have enough complications in my life at the moment."

"Platonic." He made a sour face. "Does that mean no touching whatsoever?"

"Under no circumstances."

He got up and stood behind her chair, grasping her shoulders in his hands. "What if I were to, say, give you a shoulder massage? Strictly therapeutic?"

Summer squirmed out of reach. "That would not qualify as platonic."

"Sure it would. Waiters give each other shoulder massages all the time after a long shift."

"No wonder you're so popular at the café."

"No, that would be because of my simmering sexuality and irresistible charm."

Austin reached for her shoulders again and

began to knead them with slow, deliberate strokes. It felt heavenly.

"Feels good, doesn't it?"

"No," she lied. She glanced over her shoulder nervously. From there the third-floor balcony was barely visible.

"What?" Austin asked. "Afraid someone will see you?"

"No," she lied.

"Relax. Nobody upstairs can see us through all these palms. Besides, there's nothing wrong with getting a shoulder rub, Summer. We are consenting adults." Austin bent a little closer, still kneading. "Besides, if I wanted this to go any further, I'd do something like lean close. . . ."

Summer felt his hand gently gathering her hair to one side, baring her neck. She shivered. He leaned even closer. She could feel his warm breath. She wanted to move, but she couldn't.

"Then," Austin continued in his low, soothing whisper, like wind through leaves, "then I'd brush my lips against the side of your neck, like so. . . ."

She felt the soft warmth of his mouth touching her neck. For one horrible, tantalizing moment, she almost turned to face him. A few more inches and his mouth would be on hers—

What was she *doing?* She cleared her throat.

"You know," Summer said suddenly, her voice shaky, "Seth proposed to me by a pool."

Austin laughed. "Whoa, you sure know how to dampen the mood."

"There was no mood, Austin. There's not going to be any mood."

"I believe this is called 'denial.' It's not just a river in Egypt."

"Very funny." Summer tried not to smile.

Austin ran his fingers across her shoulder blades. "If there is no mood, how come I'm still giving you a shoulder massage?"

Summer yanked free of his grasp. "You're not," she said crisply.

Austin shrugged. "Your loss. It's a great stress reducer, you know. And you're stressed out."

Summer rubbed her eyes. "You're right about that, at least. What am I going to tell Seth?"

"You realize I'm not exactly an impartial observer." Austin stroked his chin. "But if I were you, I'd probably hold off telling him. Maybe the thing'll turn up."

"I probably shouldn't take your advice, but in this case I happen to agree with you. I mean, there's no point in worrying Seth unnecessarily. In the meantime, I've got to get a job, and quick. Maybe I could earn enough to buy another one before I see him again. You think I could match it?"

"Oh, you can probably find one at any Kmart," Austin said with a laugh. "So, we still on for tomorrow? I really don't mind driving you to some interviews. Although there's always Jitters."

"I think I'll pass on Jitters." Summer hesitated. "In fact, I think I'll pass on the ride, too. I'll take the bus. Or I can wait till later and borrow Marquez's car or Diana's."

"Marquez is driving Diver back tomorrow. And you said Diana had errands to run. Let me drive you. I promise it will be entirely platonic chauffeuring. You need to start your savings account so that you can replace that ring. Although I do know a bubble gum machine where you could find a good match."

Summer stifled a smile.

"Go ahead," Austin challenged. "Laugh. I know you want to."

"I do not. I do not find you amusing."

Austin shook his head. "Yes, you do."

"You have such an ego for someone who keeps getting rejected."

For a moment Austin fell serious. His dark eyes surveyed her with longing so intense she could feel the pull of it. "I know how you really feel, Summer," he said softly. "I felt the way you kissed me over spring break. And I can wait a long time for something that good to happen again."

Summer touched his shoulder gently. "Then you're going to wait a very long time, Austin."

"You know what they say," he replied, the intensity replaced by a casual tone. "Good things come to those who wait."

14

To Be or Not to Be a File Clerk; That Is the Question

Summer awoke the next morning to a mattress that smelled like an old tennis shoe. Diana was up, her bed already made. The shower was running.

Summer padded out to the living room. Diver was on the front balcony, reading the morning paper.

"Hi," Summer said uncomfortably. "Mind if I borrow the want ads?"

She took a seat on one of the old wicker rockers the previous tenant had left behind. The morning sun was brilliant, the air filled with a rich, loamy smell from the carefully tended garden below.

Diver handed Summer the classified section. "Diana's taking a shower, I think. And Marquez is still asleep. She was kind of wired last night." He cleared his throat. On the street below, a group of tourists in gaudy T-shirts and wide-brimmed straw hats trooped by. "How did you sleep?"

"Okay. It's weird having just a mattress on the floor. It's also weird having one that smells like Grandma Smith's attic."

Diver smiled shyly. Summer studied the want ads. She felt stupid, bringing up a relative. In a strange way, it didn't feel as if she and Diver were related anymore.

"Remember that time—" Diver ran his fingers through his shimmering blond hair. "Remember that time you and I watched the sunrise on the stilt house roof?"

Summer nodded. "I remember."

"It was the best sunrise I ever saw."

"Me, too."

They fell silent. Summer scanned the ads. There wasn't much to choose from—pretty much the same stuff she'd seen advertised all week.

Just then Diana appeared on the porch. She was wearing a red velour robe and had one of her mother's towels wrapped around her head. Already she had on makeup.

"If I'd known you talked in your sleep, Summer, I would have roomed with Marquez." Diana leaned over the edge of the railing and inhaled the sweet-smelling air. "All night long. 'Oh, please, Austin' and 'Yes, yes, Austin.'"

"I did not!" Summer cried, horrified.

Diana nodded. "Jeez, Summer. You think you know someone. . . ."

Summer felt her cheeks heating. She *had* had a dream about Austin, and a pretty juicy one at that. Could she really have—

"Oh, relax, don't look so frantic. You slept like a log. Although you do snort sometimes."

"I do not snore."

"Not *snore, snort.*" Diana made a little hog-like noise. "Don't worry. It's kind of endearing."

"You're certainly in a good mood," Diver said.

"I'm going shopping. Need I say more? But I'll be back this afternoon if you need the car for job hunting, Summer."

"That's okay. I'm covered." Summer chose not to mention her chauffeur for the day. There was no point in getting Diana started. "Here's what I've narrowed it down to. A restaurant called Kaboodles needs a lunch waitron. A pancake house on the edge of town needs one for breakfast, but I think they make you wear a frilly pink apron."

"Skip that one," Diana advised. "Pink is not your color."

"Those of us who work for a living don't pick our jobs that way," came a hoarse voice from the living room.

"Marquez!" Diana exclaimed. "You look . . . not quite human."

Marquez joined them on the porch, slouching against the ivy-covered wall. There were dark, shiny circles under her eyes. "I had a rough night."

Diana grinned at Diver.

"No, not like that," Marquez said irritably. "I just couldn't get to sleep. I was tossing and turning like crazy. Diver slept on the couch." She nudged Summer. "So, what were your other choices?"

"Oh." Summer glanced at the paper. "The newspaper needs a part-time proofreader, which could be dangerous, since it involves spelling. Oh, yeah—there's a place down the highway that needs a file clerk. Something to do with dolphins, which might be cool."

"Filing for Flipper. Take that one," Marquez advised.

"No, don't," Diana said forcefully.

Everyone looked at her in surprise.

"I mean, I know that place. The Dolphin Interactive Therapy Institute, right?"

Summer nodded. "So?"

"So it's like a really long drive from here. How would you get there? The buses aren't exactly reliable. And I think it's in this rickety building, really scuzzy-looking and . . ." Diana trailed off.

Summer and Marquez were gazing at her in bafflement.

"What gives, Diana?" Marquez asked.

Diana sighed. She wasn't going to find a way out of this. "I . . . um . . . I volunteer there."

For a moment no one spoke. "You?" Marquez demanded. "*You* volunteer?"

"It's no big deal, okay? It's just something I do."

"What do you do there, Diana?" Summer asked, as surprised as Marquez was by this revelation.

Diana shrugged off the question. "Just . . . stuff. Work with the kids. Mostly they're abused and kind of messed up. They spend time with the dolphins, and sometimes they start to open up."

Marquez's mouth was hanging open. "I don't understand. This is . . . like . . . *nice,* Diana."

Diana sighed again. "I knew I shouldn't have told you."

"I think it's fantastic, Diana," Summer said, touched by the faint blush on Diana's cheeks. Diana *never* blushed. "So I guess you wouldn't want me hanging around, huh?"

Diana adjusted the tie on her robe. "It's not like that. It's just . . . you know, it was kind of my private place. I did it all last year, too, and you guys never caught on. But I knew with us living together . . ." She sighed. "Go ahead and apply, Summer. It's not like I own the place. Anyway, I gotta get ready. I've got a full day at the mall planned."

"What's the occasion?" Marquez asked.

"You don't need an occasion to shop, Marquez. But I'm on the lookout for some traveling clothes." She started to leave, pausing in the doorway. "I'm going out to the West Coast with Mallory for a few days. She's got a big book tour, and I thought she might want some company. We're leaving tomorrow."

"Whoa, hold on." Marquez grabbed her by the sleeve. "You're spending time with your mother *deliberately?* This is too much to deal with. Somebody get me a chair."

"I've got a lap here," Diver offered.

"I'd crush you," Marquez said. She stared at Diana in disbelief. "I'm having information overload here. You volunteer with needy kids *and* you're going to hang out with your mom for no reason? Where is evil Diana? Who are you and what have you done with her?"

Diana favored her with a smile. "I can see why this would be difficult to grasp. I'm a complex woman, Marquez. Whereas you are, well, your basic one-celled organism."

"Where will you be on the West Coast, Diana?" Diver asked.

"Oh, I don't know. La-la land. Beverly Hills. Places with Armani and Donna Karan boutiques."

"Newport Beach?" Summer asked. "That's a little south of L.A."

"Is that where Seth is working?" Diana asked.

Summer nodded. "Maybe you could say hi to him. He'd probably love to see a friendly face."

"I don't know," Diana said. "There probably won't be much time. But for you, I'll give it a try."

Marquez eyed Diana doubtfully. "Suddenly she's Mother Teresa. Man, I need a cup of coffee. You are definitely full of surprises, Diana."

On the street below, someone honked. Austin pulled up in an old red Karmann Ghia convertible. "Your chariot awaits," he called.

Diana smiled coolly at Summer. "It seems," she said, "I'm not the only one who's full of surprises."

Summer slumped into the passenger seat of Austin's car. It was noon, and the sun was merciless. "Well, so far I'm oh-for-four. At this rate I really will have to pick up shifts at Jitters. Although they'd probably tell me I'm underqualified. Or overqualified. Or they'll keep my application on file. Or tell me to come back next week when the manager's in . . ."

She lay back against the headrest. The sun beat down on her face. Her skirt was damp and wrinkled. Her blouse stuck to her back. Her shoes hurt. There was no way around the fact that job hunting was a full-time job. And the pay was lousy.

She cast a furtive glance at Austin. He was wearing cutoffs and no shoes, and a pair of near-black Oakleys was hiding his eyes. He'd taken off his shirt to soak up the sizzling rays. He was even more firm and well muscled than she remembered from spring break.

Austin started up the car. "What did the dolphin people say?"

"When I told them I was Diana's cousin, they couldn't stop raving about her. About how great she is with the kids, and all the progress she's made with some of their really tough cases." Summer kicked off her shoes and propped her feet on the dash. "It's weird. It's like this whole other side of Diana she's never shown to anyone."

Austin pulled onto the two-lane highway and headed back toward Coconut Key. The hot wind whipped their hair into a frenzy. "She's a strange girl, Diana. Very complex. There's something not quite trustworthy about her that makes her quite appealing."

"What do you mean? I trust her."

"Well, you know her better than I do, obviously. I just get the feeling that with Diana, there's always a little bit more to the story."

Summer watched the sea grass zipping past. The ocean was alive with sunlight. Even with sunglasses, she had to squint.

She thought about Diana's impromptu visit to California. It occurred to her that if Diana saw Seth, she might unintentionally slip and mention the lost ring . . . or even Austin. The very thought made Summer queasy. Maybe she should say something to Diana, just to be sure. Of course, chances were that Diana wouldn't even see Seth. Summer was probably worrying for nothing.

"So, anyway," Austin said, "think there's any chance the dolphin guys will hire you?"

"Oh, they were really nice, but I doubt it. Besides, I don't want to invade Diana's turf, you know? And we already live together. Working together . . . that might just be too much togetherness." Summer closed her eyes to the bone-melting sun. "And anyway, they have about a zillion applicants, and they were hoping for someone who could work part-time this fall. And I won't exactly be in commuting distance come September."

"Where *will* you be this fall, exactly?"

Summer opened her eyes. Austin was looking at her, but with his dark shades, she couldn't read his expression.

"I'll be a freshman at the University of Wisconsin."

"And why is that?"

Summer sat up a little straighter. "Because it's where I want to go to school."

"And why is that?"

"What are you all of a sudden, Joe Shrink?" Summer asked.

Austin shrugged. "Just curious."

"I'm going to UW because Seth and I were

both accepted there, and it's a good school, and it's close to my home." She hesitated. "My home" sounded funny now that she was living in Florida again. But Minnesota was her real home. It was the place where her family was, the place where she'd been born. The place she'd grown up.

"Why UW?" Austin pressed. "Why not, I don't know, the University of Minnesota? Or Michigan? Or Arkansas?"

Summer occupied herself putting her sandals back on. "Well, I did apply to some other schools. But Seth's dad and grandfather went to UW. It was kind of important to him to continue the tradition. And I didn't care where I went as long as—"

Austin looked over, lowering his shades to make sure she saw his skeptical expression. "As long as you were with Seth. That's so fifties of you. You're deciding the future of your education based on the desires of your boyfriend?" He shook his head. "You seem like such a nineties feminist. And now you reveal this dark side."

"I *am* a feminist," Summer said, scowling. "And it's not just my boyfriend. My family's there, and the friends I grew up with. My best friend in Bloomington, Jennifer, is going to UW. Lots of people I know. Not just Seth."

"And what will you be studying way up there in Wisconsin? Going for a Ph.D. in moo-cows?"

"I'm undecided." Summer crossed her arms over her chest. "How should I know what I want to be? I'm only eighteen."

"That, at least," Austin said with a grin, "is an enlightened answer."

"I'm so glad you approve."

"So the plan is, you go to UW, marry Seth, get a nice, bland job, maybe in the insurance industry—yeah, that'd be about right—then have nice, bland little Seths and Summers?"

"Something like that. Except for the insurance part. And the bland part."

They slowed as they neared the edge of Coconut Key. The town sprouted out of nowhere, a sudden, crazy hodgepodge of old houses with tin roofs and latticework porches. Many were on stilts or concrete pilings as a protection against hurricanes. Graceful herons walked the edge of the road in stately slow motion.

"So where else did you apply?"

"Some other schools in the Midwest," Summer said. "And one down here, just for the hell of it."

"Florida Coastal? The one Diana and Marquez are going to?"

Summer shook her head.

"Carlson?" Austin looked at her with renewed respect. "Isn't that a private experimental college?"

"It was just an idea. My English teacher suggested it. She said it would stimulate me or something like that. English teachers love to talk about stimulation. The intellectual kind of stimulation, anyway."

"And you were accepted?"

"It doesn't matter, Austin. I'm not going there. I'm going to UW."

They drove on in silence for a while. Summer closed her eyes. The sun was making her drowsy.

"Hang on." Austin took a sudden, sharp turn to the right onto a small dirt road lined by squat palms.

"Where are we going?" Summer asked, grabbing the door handle to keep her balance.

"Detour."

"What kind of detour?"

"A good detour." He gave her a cryptic smile. "Most detours are."

15

Love at First Sight

"I think I'm in love," Summer murmured as she got out of the car.

"I knew you'd come to your senses eventually," Austin said.

"Not with you. With this place. Have you ever seen such a beautiful school? I mean, it looked good in the brochures. But this is amazing."

She started down a manicured stone path lined by magnificent palms.

"Wait up," Austin called, "I need to put on a shirt," but Summer couldn't wait.

Carlson's tiny campus was set at the very tip of Coconut Key. Its white stucco buildings with red tile roofs were arrayed along the beach. The grounds were thick with exotic tropical plants in full bloom. In the center of the campus was the striking student union building, a huge mansion that had once been the winter residence of R. T. Carlson, an illiterate immigrant who'd grown up to be an eccentric but generous railroad baron. Upon his death, he'd requested that the land and residence be turned into a college.

Austin fell into step beside her. "What a beautiful, strange place," he said. "Check out the huge trees over there."

"Banyan trees," Summer said. "The roots grow down to form new trunks. They're from India. My English teacher said she used to attend poetry classes under the trunks. It's like a big tree house."

"So she went to school here?"

"Ms. Desai. She said it was the best choice she ever made." Summer paused to watch two students sitting by a fountain. "It's a real free-form curriculum. You don't declare a major. Instead you just take lots of different courses based on important works of literature."

"I've heard about it. It's tough to get into." He winked at her. "No sweat for you, though, huh?"

"My grades weren't that great. They must have liked the essay I wrote."

They sat on the shady steps of the main

building. "So what was your essay about?" Austin asked, leaning back on his elbows.

"What I wanted from my education."

"And that would be . . . ?"

"Well, basically I said I wasn't sure, but that I thought if I had a good education, I would be able to make informed decisions. You know, make good choices in my life." Summer shrugged, feeling suddenly self-conscious. "Blah, blah, blah."

Austin touched her on the shoulder. "Don't make fun of yourself that way. I think that's exactly what you should want from an education."

Summer eyed him doubtfully. "If you're so pro-college, then why did you drop out of the University of Texas after only a semester?"

"Hey, do as I say, not as I do." It was Austin's turn to look uncomfortable. "I guess it was all the stuff with my dad. All of a sudden he's got this incurable disease, and there's a fifty-fifty shot I'm going to get it. Acing Rocks for Jocks just didn't seem to matter much."

"What were you going to major in?"

"Poetry." He grinned at her, a self-conscious, cockeyed grin that was sweet and self-deprecating. "Yes, I know. Business or medicine might make me more cash. No, they would *definitely* make me more cash. But my dad was a music major at Juilliard, and he turned out okay. His cello career was really taking off, until . . .

well, anyway, I'm going to go back to school. I just need some time to regroup, is all."

The heavy stained-glass doors to the union opened, and a petite young woman with a long braid down her back appeared on the top step. She was carrying a massive load of books. As she started down the steps she dropped several. Summer and Austin leapt to the rescue.

"Thanks," she said. "I think I bit off more than I can chew."

"Need a hand?" Summer asked.

"That'd be great. I'm just heading over to Wilson Hall. Thataway."

They split up the books and started down a winding path toward one of the stucco buildings near the beach.

"I'm Cary Woo," the woman said. "I'm a TA in English lit."

"What's a TA?" Summer asked.

"Teaching assistant. I'll bet you're going to be a freshman, right? I'd remember you otherwise."

"You know everybody on this campus?" Austin asked incredulously.

"It's a tiny place. Everyone knows everyone."

Austin laughed. "The University of Texas was like a small city."

"That's how UW is," Summer said. "Really big."

"Well, that has its advantages," Cary said. "Lots of variety. Me, I like the family feel of Carlson. It's a special place."

She opened the door to one of the little buildings. Big windows afforded a view of the white beach and the endless water beyond. "Plus," Cary added, "the view's spectacular. And if you want more excitement, there's always FCU, down the road. We share some facilities and library resources with them, so it's like having a sister campus."

"Two of my friends are going there." Summer dropped her load of books onto the wooden desk at the front of the classroom. The room smelled of chalk dust and sea air.

"Well, thanks for the help," Cary said.

"Anytime." Austin started for the door. "Summer? You coming?"

Summer hesitated. "Cary?" she said shyly.

"Hmm?"

"Are the classes here as hard as everybody says?"

"Oh, yeah, they're tough." She laughed. "I mean, you work your tush off here. It's intense and it's focused. It's not the right college for everybody. You have to be very self-motivated, very into learning." She paused. "But it's worth it. It's something you'll take with you the rest of your life. It helps you define where you want to go, to make the right choices, you know?"

Summer glanced over her shoulder at Austin. He was leaning against the doorjamb, thumbs hooked in his pockets, studying her carefully.

"Yeah," Summer said. "I guess."

A few steps out the door, Summer stopped in midstride.

"What?" Austin asked.

"Just a second. Wait here, okay?" She ran back to the doorway. "Cary?"

Cary looked up in surprise. "Back already?"

"I was wondering . . . if someone had applied here and been accepted but then said no and then decided she wanted to maybe go after all, what would that someone do?"

Cary smiled. "I imagine that someone would check in with admissions," she said.

"That's what I figured."

"Good luck," Cary said.

Summer nodded. "It's really hard here, huh?"

"It's really great, too."

Austin was waiting for her under a palm tree. "Forget something?"

"Not exactly," Summer said softly. "I may have overlooked something, though."

"Mind if I swing by my place?" Austin asked when they returned to his car. "I've got to work tonight, and I need to pick up my waitron clothes."

Summer looked at him doubtfully.

"Believe me, it's not a place for seduction, Summer. It's pretty much of a hellhole."

"Okay, then."

Austin's apartment wasn't a hellhole, but it did make Summer's place look palatial. It was a garage apartment, a tiny one-bedroom on a side street in the seedier part of Coconut Key.

"I've never seen so many books outside the library," Summer said, stepping over a cardboard box full of musty-smelling volumes.

"I had my mom ship them out. Cost me a fortune. But they're like friends, you know? I felt lost without them around." He yanked off his T-shirt. "Make yourself at home. I've gotta change. There might be something edible in the fridge, but I wouldn't put money on it. If it's moving, don't eat it."

Summer sat on the aging couch. She felt guilty being in Austin's apartment, although there was really no reason for her to feel that way. She picked up a volume of poetry off the floor. Rilke. One of Cary's books had been a volume of poetry.

Summer tried to picture herself sitting in one of Carlson's white stucco buildings. She would be carrying a heavy book bag. All her fellow students would be smarter. She would ask stupid questions, and they would be too polite to laugh, but they would snicker behind their hands.

Austin reappeared. He'd changed into his work clothes and run a comb through his windblown hair. He looked way too good to be going to a job waiting tables. He looked way too good for Summer to be in his apartment without a chaperon.

"Sorry I can't feed you. How about tomorrow night, though? It's my birthday. I could cook you up some lasagna or something."

"I don't think so, Austin."

He shook his head. "You're going to make me spend my birthday alone in this hovel? Have you no heart?"

She hesitated. "A platonic birthday dinner? No strings?"

"No strings. Just the best lasagna you've ever tasted."

"I guess." She fell silent, staring at the Rilke book she was holding.

"You're awfully quiet."

"I was thinking about that school."

Austin sat beside her. "You're thinking about reapplying, aren't you?"

Summer stared at him, aghast. "I didn't say that."

"You implied it. Implied applying." He touched her hand. "You are, aren't you?"

She closed her eyes. "Everyone is counting on my going to UW. Seth. My mom. Jennifer. All my high school friends. I have a dorm room picked out. I put a deposit down. It's too late to change my mind."

"It's never too late, Summer. Never."

Summer groaned. "How can I be so unsure about everything? How could I not know? I made a decision, and I have to stick with it."

"You made a decision based on inadequate information. You chose UW without seeing Carlson. Today you went there, and it felt right, didn't it?"

Summer nodded. "But I can't change my mind just because the campus is pretty."

"That's not why it felt right. It felt right because you saw yourself there and you realized you'd let your fear get in the way of making the right choice. You talked to Cary and you started to think, 'Hey, I could make it here.'"

"I'm not smart enough for Carlson."

Austin looked annoyed. "I guess the admissions people were just hitting the beer pretty heavy on the day your application showed up."

Summer rubbed the spot where her ring should have been. "I can't. What about my mom? She needs me right now. What about Seth? He's counting on our being together. I can't."

"I know you think I'm biased here, and I am." Austin took her fidgeting hands and held them still. "But you have to believe me when I tell you that you can't make decisions about your life because it will make your mom happy or some guy happy. Not even," he added with a sigh, "if that guy is me."

"I know that."

"But do you really?"

Summer thought of the classroom again. She pictured Cary asking her a question. Maybe a question about Keats, a difficult question, an unfathomably hard question, not at all like questions Ms. Desai had asked all year in senior English.

She pictured herself answering the question. No one in the class would smile. She would answer correctly. They would all be impressed. They would see that she had valuable things to offer. They would know that she belonged.

"If I could be wrong about college," Summer whispered, "I could be wrong about . . . anything."

Austin nodded. "Welcome to life," he said.

He was leaning toward her so imperceptibly that his lips were almost on hers before she realized that this time they really were going to kiss.

It was as if they'd kissed a million times, and as if they'd never kissed before. It was as if Austin knew just what she was feeling. It was as if he'd climbed right inside her mind and her heart to a place she'd never let anyone go before.

It was as if he'd seen the part of her that knew all the right answers.

16

Dangerous Pictures, Dangerous Pills

When Diana got home from shopping, the apartment was empty. It was also hot, stuffy, and an incredible mess. Cardboard boxes were stacked everywhere. Crumpled newspaper littered the floor. One of Marquez's bras was stuck between the couch cushions. A stack of dirty dishes leaned precariously in the sink.

Was it any wonder Summer had lost her engagement ring in this chaos? Of course, Diana knew, there was a psychological element to it, too. It was way too symbolic, given Summer's flirtation with Austin, for it not to have been.

Diana tossed her shopping bags onto the couch. A skirt, two tops, a dress, a pair of shorts, some silver earrings, and the pack of photos from the one-hour lab at the mall. The only thing she hadn't gotten around to was picking up some shoes.

She checked her watch. Well, she could at least try calling him. There was a chance he'd be home from work by that time. Diana would have to get Seth's number from Summer's address book.

She rummaged through the pile of stuff next to Summer's bed and finally located the little blue address book. Summer had drawn red hearts around Seth's name. How very cute, Diana thought. How very cute and insincere. She copied Seth's number and address down on a piece of scrap paper and put the address book back where she'd found it.

Her eyes fell on a pair of Summer's shoes, brand-new leather ones with chunky lug soles that would look great with the black micromini Diana had just bought at Burdine's that afternoon. Would it be tacky to borrow your cousin's never-worn shoes while you were borrowing her slightly used boyfriend?

Diana slipped her foot into the right shoe. It was a little snug, but she could get by for a night if she had to. She tried on the other one. Her toe hit something hard, like a piece of metal.

Frowning, Diana took off the shoe and felt inside.

The minute she touched it, she knew she'd hit gold. Literally.

She pulled out the ring and held it up to the light.

It was too bad Diana didn't believe in signs. Because this one was a neon-lit, bigger-than-life, in-your-face sign if she'd ever heard of one.

She grabbed her cell phone, stretched out on her bed, and dialed the number she'd copied out of Summer's address book.

She slipped the ring onto her finger. She could not seem to stop smiling.

For a giddy second she thought about putting everything on the line, just telling Seth there and then how she felt. She never really had, except in those letters she hadn't had the guts to mail.

Wait, she told herself. Savor it. She had to wait till the time was right. In romance, timing was everything.

"Seth?" she said when he answered on the second ring. "You'll never guess who this is."

It was only two flights of stairs from Jitters to the apartment, but Marquez felt as though she were climbing Everest. She must have gained weight, must have. How else could she explain this heaviness in her limbs? Her legs and arms felt like big sacks of flour.

She'd worked her butt off at lunch and even

stayed late, but still she'd only made a lousy sixteen bucks in tips. She was never going to make it through the school year this way. Maybe she could find a classier place to work or take on some more shifts. Maybe even pick up a second job for the summer.

At the door to the apartment, she fumbled for her key. Her hands had been shaking all day. Her breath came in sharp gasps. She definitely had gained weight. She was going to have to buy a new scale—if she could ever come up with the spare cash.

It was hot inside, and dark. The louvered doors were closed. She heard a muffled voice coming from the room Summer and Diana shared. The bedroom door was closed.

She wondered if the phone had been installed yet. But no, that was supposed to happen next week. It must be someone on Diana's cell phone.

Curious, Marquez put her ear to the door.

"Oh, come on, Seth. For old times' sake."

Diana? Talking to Seth?

"We had fun over New Year's, didn't we?"

Marquez leaned a little too hard on the door, making it rattle. Instantly Diana yanked it open. The phone was in her hand.

"Oh," she said, looking immensely relieved, "it's you. I thought maybe it was Summer. What were you doing? Eavesdropping?"

"I was just wondering who you were talking to, is all."

"When did you get home?"

"Just now." Marquez pointed to the phone. "Is that Seth?"

"Um, yeah. I was just . . . um, letting him know I'll be out west with Mallory. You know. In case we could all get together."

"You and Mallory and Seth."

"Yeah. You know, for dinner or something." Diana shoved the phone at her. "You wanna say hi?"

"I'm kind of beat. You tell him hi for me."

"Sure. I will." Quickly Diana shut the door behind her.

Marquez went to her room. Very strange, she thought as she shed her waitron clothes for her exercise gear. Diana's acting as though she'd been caught with her hand in the cookie jar. Marquez sometimes wondered if maybe there wasn't something a little odd going on between Seth and Diana.

Marquez tied on her sneakers. It wasn't anything she could put her finger on. Certainly not the kind of thing she'd ever mention to Summer, who had a vivid imagination when it came to problems of any stripe.

In the kitchen, Marquez surveyed the cupboard. She'd skipped breakfast and lunch, which was good, because she was clearly putting on the pounds again. She got out a piece of bread, a knife, and a plate. Carefully she sliced the bread into four squares. She sliced each of those squares into four more pieces.

She could hear Diana's laughter in the other room. It was probably nothing. And if it wasn't, Marquez didn't want to know about it. She had enough on her mind without getting into some mess between Diana and Summer.

She picked up one of the squares, placed it on her tongue, and hesitated. Just two. She would eat only two of the tiny squares. The rest she would save for dinner.

Marquez ate the bread very slowly. She put the other squares in a plastic bag and took it to her bedroom. In her top dresser drawer there were two other bags, each with their own squares of bread. She'd been good those times. She hadn't eaten any of the extra squares.

She'd just climbed onto her exercise bike when Diana emerged from her bedroom, looking flushed and hyper.

"So," Diana said energetically, "want to see what I bought today?"

"Not unless you got a bathroom scale," Marquez said. Slowly she began pedaling. Her legs did not want to cooperate.

Diana sat on the couch, studying Marquez as if she were an exotic zoo animal. "Didn't you just get off work?"

"Yeah, and I'm picking up a dinner shift tonight."

"Did you have lunch? There's some pizza in the fridge we could nuke."

"I already ate."

Diana frowned. "Marquez, I know you don't want advice from me—"

"You got that right."

"—but don't you think maybe you're overdoing it? The dieting and the exercising and working extra shifts."

"Not all of us can spend our days running up the credit cards, Diana," Marquez muttered. "Some of us have to work for a living." She was annoyed at the sound of jealousy in her own voice.

"If you need money—"

"I don't need money. As it happens, I still owe you from that credit card I used over spring break."

"Don't worry about that, Marquez."

"Look, Diana, I'm going to pay you back every penny, one way or another." Marquez pedaled harder. Sweat poured off her brow, and she'd barely started.

Diana opened the front porch doors to let in more breeze. "You look kind of worn out, to tell you the truth, Marquez. Your parents just moved, and you're working really hard. That can be awfully stressful."

"Did you learn that at your dolphin job? What, did they make you an honorary psychologist?"

Diana looked annoyed, to Marquez's satisfaction. She was silent for a few blissful minutes. Then she started in again.

"We've had a couple of girls there . . ." Diana pursed her lips, as if she wasn't sure whether to continue. "Girls with, you know, dieting problems. There's a woman who works with them, a counselor who's really cool. I could give you her name."

Marquez stopped pedaling. She could feel the anger moving inside her like a caged animal. "Are you suggesting I need a shrink because I'm trying to lose a few pounds?"

"It's not just a few pounds, Marquez. And maybe you can fool your family and Summer, but I'm around you more. I'm just saying that I could give you her name if you wanted to talk. I'd pay for it, too."

Marquez sent Diana her steeliest gaze. "I do not need your help running my life, Diana. If we're going to be sharing this apartment, let's get that straight right now. I'm not going to pry into your complicated little mind. I'm not going to ask why you're calling your cousin's fiancé. I'm not going to, because I've got my own life to keep track of, and that's hard enough. All right?"

Diana held up her hands. "Okay, okay. You're right. I'm sorry." She gave a shrug. "What do I know, anyway? I do a little volunteer work now and then, and suddenly I think I'm Sigmund Freud."

She headed for her room. "Just for the record, there's nothing going on between Seth and me." She smiled frostily. "But you're right. It's none of your business, anyway."

17

Summer Goes to Dreamland, and Diana Goes to La-La Land

Summer checked her alarm clock. Three-twenty in the morning. Diana was snoring very loudly. And she claimed Summer made noise!

She rolled off her mattress and made her way across the floor, nearly tripping on an open suitcase. Diana was leaving early that morning for California. Aunt Mallory was picking her up, and Diana had been nice enough to say Summer could use Diana's car while she was gone.

Summer gently closed the door behind her. Marquez's door was shut. The main room was striped by yellow moonlight coursing through the louvered doors. The air was hot and sticky, even for a June night.

She located Diana's cell phone under a pile

of clothes. Carefully she punched in the numbers. Please, please, please, let it be Seth who answers, she thought. It wasn't as late in California, but he and his roommates got up early for work.

To her relief, the sleepy voice at the other end was Seth's.

"Hi, it's me, Summer," she whispered. "Did I wake you?"

"No." Seth yawned. "Well, okay, yes. But I'm glad you did. Is anything wrong?"

She sat on the couch, hugging her knees. "Not really. I just wanted to talk, is all."

For a sudden, vivid moment, she flashed back to that afternoon and the way she'd felt in Austin's arms. Guilt washed over her like an icy wave.

"This isn't about, uh, Diana, is it?"

"Diana? No, why?"

"Nothing. I was just wondering."

"She's coming out to California this weekend with my aunt. There probably won't be time, but I thought I'd give her your address, you know, in case they can stop by. Would that be okay?"

"Um, sure." There was a long pause. "Yeah, that'd be okay."

"I don't have to if you don't want. I could just tell her you're really tied up with work. I know Diana can be kind of . . . well, Diana."

"It's okay," Seth said, sounding a little edgy. "Whatever."

"You're tired. I should let you go back to sleep."

"No, don't go," Seth said quickly. "Don't go yet. I like just hearing your voice. What did you do today?"

"I went job hunting." With Austin. "Then I stopped by that college we applied to, Carlson." With Austin. Then I kissed Austin till I thought I'd pass out.

"What's it like?"

"Carlson? I thought it was pretty cool. I met a teacher there. A teaching assistant, really. She said it's true what they say about it being a tough curriculum."

"I'm glad I didn't get in, then," Seth said. "We want to have some fun during college, after all."

"What if . . ." Summer took a deep breath. "What do you think would have happened to us if we'd decided to go to different colleges? You know, like Mindy Burke and Joe McGrath? You think we would have been able to pull it off?"

"I don't know. It was hard enough with me living just a couple of hours away from you in Wisconsin. I can't imagine doing that for four years straight, can you?"

"No." Summer bit her lip. "I guess not."

Seth yawned again.

"We should hang up," Summer said. "I just wanted to hear your voice for a minute. Sometimes it feels like you're so far away, and I feel so lost, you know?"

"I know. Me, too. But it won't be forever."

Summer felt a hot tear make its way down her cheek. "I love you, Seth," she whispered, and then she hung up before she started crying.

She lay on the couch, sobbing softly into the smelly old cushions, hoping she wouldn't wake Diana or Marquez. She didn't want to have to explain herself. She didn't want to try to explain how she was torn between two guys—one the safe and sweet choice, the other challenging and passionate.

Or how she was torn between two colleges—one the comfortable and simple choice, the other difficult and even scary.

She was even torn, she suddenly realized, between two places. The place where she'd grown up, where her family and long-term friends were, where the winters were bitter and the summers brief, and her adopted home there in the Keys, where the summers were sweltering but the sun never, ever stopped shining.

She closed her eyes and fell into a fitful, uneasy sleep.

She dreamed that she was in a classroom at Carlson. There was only one other student present—Austin. He was standing at the board, wearing his Jitters T-shirt, writing down an equation that explained the complex physics principles involved in the act of kissing. Summer tried to keep up, but she kept getting confused:

```
x/y
2(x-y) x (Summer - Seth)
Austin = the right answer
```

Every time she raised her hand to get help, the telephone in her book bag would ring. And every time she answered it, it was Seth, wanting to know what she'd done with her engagement ring.

She got a lousy night's sleep.

Diana tiptoed out of the bedroom around six o'clock. Summer, for some reason, was sprawled out on the couch, softly snorting, as usual.

Well, no point in waking her. Quick, clean getaways were always the best.

Diana sneaked past the couch, her suitcase in tow. She stole another guilty glance at her cousin. She was a beautiful girl, in the wholesome, sunny way that guys like Seth always fell for. She looked so sweet and guileless that Diana felt an annoying twinge of remorse.

It wasn't as though she hadn't tried to keep

Summer and Seth together, she reminded herself. Summer was the one who'd allowed Austin back into her life. Summer was the one who'd blown her chance with Seth.

Diana eased open the door. She could wait for Mallory, who would undoubtedly be late, down at Jitters, maybe have herself a latte and a cinnamon roll.

The door creaked like something out of a bad horror movie. Summer stirred instantly.

"Diana? Are you leaving already?"

"Yep. See you in a couple of days. The car keys are on my dresser."

Diana scooted out the door, but it was too late.

"Hey, wait."

She set down her bag with a sigh. "I'm kind of in a hurry, Summer."

"Sorry. I was just thinking you might want Seth's number and address, in case you have time."

Damn. Diana hesitated. She could let it go, pretend she hadn't called Seth, but Marquez might spill it.

"Not necessary. I called him yesterday to see if he'd be around."

"You did?" Summer sat up, rubbing her eyes. "But I just talked to him last night, and he didn't mention it."

Diana studied her manicured nails. "Well,

we just touched base for a sec. He probably forgot, is all."

"Maybe."

"Hey, I borrowed your black shoes. Is that okay?"

"Sure. We're roommates. What's mine is yours."

Diana cleared her throat. "Well, I gotta run. Good luck with the job hunt—"

"Listen, one other thing." Now Summer looked fully awake, even wary. "If you do see Seth—"

"I probably won't. There won't be a lot of time, and you know Mallory—"

"But if you *do,* do me a favor and don't mention Austin. It would just worry Seth. You know how he is."

"I don't see why you'd care. It's not like there's anything going on between you and Austin, right?"

"Just don't mention him, all right?" Summer said pointedly.

"You know me better than that, Summer." Diana grabbed her bag. "Gotta run."

"And Diana? The same thing goes for the ring, right? I mean, who knows, it may still turn up."

Diana gave a fleeting smile. "It wouldn't surprise me at all."

18

Summer Makes a Call while Diana Pays a Call

"You've been staring at that cell phone for hours, Summer," Marquez chided that afternoon. "Lift your feet, by the way. I'm in full sweep mode."

"Would you please stop cleaning already?" Summer pulled her feet up onto the couch so Marquez could rush past with a broom. "You're making me feel guilty."

"This place is a sty."

"Yeah, but since when is that an issue for you? Your old room was never exactly neat, Marquez. I remember one time it took you three days to locate your bed."

Marquez whisked dirt into a dustpan with frantic little strokes. "This is different. There are three of us slobs now. Although, to be fair,

Diana is truly the queen of crap." She pointed toward a pile of cardboard boxes stacked against one wall. "Look at all that stuff. She's just waiting for the maid to show up."

Summer smiled wryly. "You're the next best thing."

"I work cheap, that's for sure."

"Are you okay, Marquez? You look kind of run-down."

"Did you and Diana get together and decide to gang up on me?" Marquez demanded, hands on hips. "Because I really do not need two extra mothers, thank you very much."

"Why? Did Diana say something?"

"Something along the lines of 'Stop working so hard, stop exercising and dieting so much,' which is way easy advice, coming from a rich, skinny, lazy person."

Summer could tell she'd hit a nerve. Maybe she'd back off, talk to Diana about it when she got back. She could even talk to Diver, although that would be kind of awkward. One thing was sure: There was no reasoning with Marquez when she got like this. It would be better to let her cool off, then try her again on a calmer day.

Summer made a space on the couch. "Come sit with me, Marquez. You could use a break. And I need advice."

"No offense, but I'd rather clean the sink."

"Okay, compromise. You clean the sink *and* give me advice."

Marquez grabbed a sponge and a can of Comet. "Does this have something to do with that phone you've been flirting with all day?"

Summer nodded. "I've been thinking about switching colleges. Going to Carlson instead of UW."

Marquez dropped her sponge, blinking in disbelief. "But that would be fantastic, Summer! Diana and I would be just down the street at FCU, and maybe we could even keep this place! And we'd all be together this fall—" She stopped in midsentence. "Uh-oh," she said, her voice hushed. "Seth."

"Seth," Summer repeated. She closed her eyes and groaned. "I feel like such a ditz, Marquez. I mean, I made a commitment to UW. And Seth and my mom and Jennifer and everybody back home, they're all counting on me. But when I visited Carlson yesterday, I realized how special it was. And the only reason I didn't pursue going there was because Seth didn't get in." She sighed. "No, that's not the only reason. I was afraid I couldn't cut it there. It's really tough, and I was sure I'd fail."

"And now you're not so sure?" Marquez asked.

"Now I'm starting to wonder how I'd feel if I never even gave it a chance. But I don't know how to choose, Marquez. If I was wrong about UW, I could be wrong about everything."

Marquez picked up her sponge and occupied herself with the sink, scrubbing diligently. After a while she turned to face Summer. "This isn't about Austin, is it? About being close to him? I mean, you *are* doing birthday lasagna tonight."

"Platonic birthday lasagna," Summer corrected. She hadn't told Marquez about the unfortunate kiss incident. She was trying to convince herself it hadn't happened.

"Whatever kind of lasagna," Marquez said. "The point is, does this change of heart have anything to do with him?"

"No. I asked myself that, but no. It isn't even about you and Diana, or about staying here in Florida. I'm starting to realize I have to make decisions based on what I feel in my heart, not what will make everybody else happy." She clutched one of the stained old couch pillows. "Besides, no matter what I do, it'll be a mess. It's too late to make everybody happy. So that kind of just leaves me. But I'm not sure I have the guts to go through with it. Assuming, that is, Carlson will even consider my application this late."

"Well, how will you feel if you don't do it?" Marquez asked gently.

"I'll feel like I was afraid to do the hard thing. Like I was afraid of failing. And that feels awful. But disappointing people because I'm confused and stupid and indecisive and idiotic, that feels awful, too."

Marquez set her sponge aside. "You are none of those things. Well, except maybe indecisive. And confused." She retrieved a small framed picture off the counter. "Here's my advice," she said, handing it to Summer. "Me and e.e., whoever he is."

Summer stared for a long time at the poem Austin had given her. "If I say yes to this, I'm saying no to so many other things."

"Like Seth. What will you do about him?" Marquez asked gravely.

Summer swallowed. Her throat was tight and dry. "Hope he understands? Visit him on holidays?"

"And what will you do about Austin?"

"I don't need to do anything about Austin. There's nothing that needs doing where Austin's concerned."

Marquez shook her head. "Sometimes I'm really glad I'm me and not you, Summer. Not usually. But sometimes." She hesitated for a moment. "Listen—" She hesitated.

"What?"

"Oh, nothing."

"What, Marquez?"

Marquez shrugged. "I was just wondering if you knew that Diana called Seth yesterday."

"Yeah, she mentioned it this morning, when she was leaving."

"Oh." Marquez looked relieved. "Good."

"Why?"

"No reason. Just wondering, is all." She motioned to the phone. "Go ahead. Call the college before you lose your nerve."

Summer took a deep breath, then called information. "Could I have the number for Carlson College?" she asked.

She punched in the number. "Why does it have to be so complicated, Marquez?" she asked as the phone rang.

Marquez gave a dark laugh. "Girl," she said, shaking her head, "you are most definitely asking the wrong person."

Diana parked the rental car in front of a nondescript apartment building on the outskirts of Newport Beach. She checked the directions Seth had given her when she'd called him from her hotel room. Yep, she was in the right place. So why did she feel so wrong?

She checked herself out in the rearview mirror. A little more lip gloss, a touch-up with her brush. She was stalling, and she knew it. She wondered if Seth was watching her from one of the windows. He'd sounded neutral on the phone. Not encouraging, exactly, but not as though he was sending her definite "back off" signals either. He'd sounded like she felt: unsure.

Diana dropped her brush back into her purse. The packet of pictures was tucked inside. So was Summer's ring, in a little zippered pouch. Diana opened it and felt a shot of courage. Her secret weapon.

Summer's disloyalty was the reason this was okay. Summer didn't deserve Seth. Summer didn't want Seth.

She'd had her chance. Now it was Diana's turn.

Slowly Diana got out of the car. She looked good in her black mini and the shoes she'd borrowed from Summer. That was something, anyway. It should have given her confidence. Usually she approached guys with the secret knowledge that they were silently swooning over her. But with Seth, she couldn't be sure.

Before she could even knock, he appeared behind the screen door. She couldn't quite read his face through the screen.

"Diana," Seth said softly.

He opened the door, and she wrapped her arms around his neck and gave him a kiss—on the lips, yes, but nothing to scare him off. Just a taste of the possibilities, a reminder of what he'd been missing. His arms were harder than she remembered. He seemed taller, too.

Seth pulled away awkwardly, leaving her dizzy and disoriented. He took a couple of steps back. "I, uh, I thought we'd maybe go get something to eat. You hungry?"

"Starved. That sounds great."

"I just need to grab my wallet and some shoes." He combed his fingers through his thick chestnut hair. "Did you have any trouble getting here?"

Diana clutched her purse a little tighter. "If you only knew, Seth," she said lightly. "If you only knew."

19

You Learn the Most Interesting Things When You Clean House

"You're late," Austin admonished as he held open the door. He had a kitchen towel draped over one shoulder and a wooden spoon in his right hand. "I was starting to worry."

"Sorry." Summer slipped inside. "I was debating whether to come."

Austin frowned. "Scared of my cooking? Or of me?"

"Both." Summer handed him the envelope she was carrying. "Happy birthday."

"It's either a check or a gift certificate. Just the right thing to send the message 'I care, but not a whole lot.'"

Summer headed for the kitchen, which smelled of tangy tomato sauce and garlic. "It's from the bookstore. I thought you could pick out a book you really wanted. You've got so many, and I didn't want to get you something you already had."

"Thanks," Austin said, sounding genuinely pleased. "It's the perfect present." He grinned. "Even if it is cold and impersonal."

Summer peeked in the oven. "Looks good."

"And only slightly burned."

As she stood, Austin slipped his arms around her. "Austin," Summer said firmly, "this is a platonic birthday meal, remember?"

He looked at her incredulously. "And was that a platonic kiss yesterday?"

"Look, I think we need to talk. How about a beach walk?"

Austin hooked his thumbs in his pockets. "Sure, why not? We'll work up a big appetite, which might not be a bad idea, given my culinary skills. Just let me go throw on a shirt without tomato sauce on it."

While Austin was changing, the phone in the living room rang. "Want me to get it?" Summer asked.

"Naw," Austin called from the bedroom. "Let the machine do the dirty work."

A moment later his answering machine clicked on. A soft voice, an older, more muted version of Austin's, filled the room. Summer felt uncomfortable listening, but there was nowhere to go to avoid it.

"Hey, it's me, your much older, much wiser sibling. I hope you're not picking up 'cause you've got better things to do, hopefully better things involving someone of the female persuasion. Let's see, what's up . . . I talked to Mom last week. Dad's worse, no surprise, but enough of that. Seriously, give me a call sometime, okay? I'm worried about you. The news hits hard for a while, I know. Let me know how you're holding up, Austin. It gets easier after a while, really it does. Anyway, have a good one. Happy nineteenth. There'll be many more. Believe me, there will."

The room went quiet. Austin appeared in the doorway, his face expressionless.

"Was that your brother?" Summer asked.

"Yeah." Austin brushed past her toward the door. "You ready?"

"What did he mean, 'Let me know how you're holding up'?"

"Who knows?" Austin held open the door. "He downs a couple of beers, he gets sentimental."

"And when he said it gets easier—"

"You know, my dad. He was talking about my dad, Summer. Now can we go already?" Austin snapped.

"Sorry."

"No, I'm sorry." Austin rubbed his eyes. "It's just birthdays. They give me the creeps. I always feel like I have to live up to the high standards of happiness set by society."

"A walk on the beach followed by lasagna," Summer said, heading out into the soft night air. "That's not so bad for your nineteenth birthday, is it?"

Austin closed the door behind him and gazed up at the sky. "Platonic lasagna," he corrected. "Technically, it could be better."

Marquez grabbed the last two cardboard boxes and carried them into Diana's bedroom. The slob. It was a good thing Marquez had energy to burn. It was her day off, and she'd spent it in high gear, scrubbing and dusting and rearranging. The amazing thing was, she still had energy left. Maybe it was the pills. Or maybe it was because she'd eaten virtually nothing all day. No fat calories or carbohydrates to drag her down. She was practically floating around the apartment. If it weren't for her megabutt, she'd quite possibly be flying.

Near Diana's bed, she felt a little dizzy. The ceiling swirled and the floor buckled. She let the boxes tumble to the floor and dropped onto the edge of the bed.

Letters and papers covered the floor like snow. Damn. Now she'd have to clean up even more of Diana's mess.

She put her head in her hands and waited for

the dizziness to pass. It wasn't the first time. It had been happening more and more. At first it had scared her. But soon Marquez had realized it was a sign she was being good. It meant she was really accomplishing her goal. She could *feel* herself getting lighter. If her head felt light, could her body be far behind? She almost liked the dizzy feeling, the way it passed through her like a shimmering white wave of pure energy.

Out in the backyard, she could hear people splashing in the pool. Blythe and some friends. They'd asked Marquez to join them, but she'd lied and claimed Diver was coming over. The truth was, he was working late that night, but Marquez was okay with that. Lately she didn't much care about being around other people. They just got in the way, asked questions, gave her disapproving looks.

Marquez paused for a minute to count up her calories for the last twenty-four hours. She'd never been good at math, but somehow she'd developed the ability to compute calories down to the last piece of gum or carrot stick. It was a weird skill. It was a shame there weren't more career opportunities in calorie counting.

She tallied up the day and considered. Not bad, not great. If she didn't eat anything that night, she'd be doing okay.

Slowly Marquez got on her knees to scoop up the letters and papers she'd dropped. What a pack rat Diana was! Like anyone cared about her junior-year essay on *Silas Marner.* There were endless postcards as well, all from Diana's mother on her book tours, scribbled illegibly in red pen, not that Marquez cared what they said.

Marquez's mother had written her just once since moving. It had been on a piece of plain white paper in pencil, a busy note full of anecdotes about the family. At the bottom she'd written,

Are you eating enough and taking your vitamins? Remember how much your mama loves you, Maria. Marquez had tucked the letter inside her pillowcase. When she tossed and turned at night, she liked knowing it was there.

As she piled the last of the letters into their cardboard container, an odd return address on an envelope caught Marquez's eye. Why would Diana have kept a letter she'd written to somebody else?

Then Marquez saw the intended recipient: Seth Warner.

Marquez withdrew the letter from its envelope, feeling a weird mix of curiosity, indifference, and guilt. Her hands were trembling, the way they always seemed to lately. It was really annoying when she was trying to pour coffee. She'd come close to scalding several customers at Jitters.

The date at the top of the letter made her

blink. January fourteenth of that year. Just a few days after Marquez and Diana had visited Summer and Diver and Seth over winter vacation.

She started to read. The handwriting was precise and feminine, but the letters kept blurring together, and Marquez had to stop and close her eyes several times.

1/14

Seth:

This is my fifth letter to you. You haven't received any of them because I haven't sent any of them, and I probably won't send this one either. I'm not used to embarrassing myself, and I'm not used to being the one doing the chasing. Face it, I'm used to guys coming after me. This is a new experience. I'm sure you're smiling to yourself right now in that smug way you sometimes have.

But anyway, here goes. I know you think what happened between us New Year's Eve was a terrible mistake. I did too, at first, because like you I care about Summer. But now that I'm back in Florida and my head has cleared, I've started to realize something. It wasn't a mistake, Seth. Those feelings have been there between us for a long time, just waiting in the shadows. And if it took breaking down on some icy highway in Minnesota for us to figure that out, then maybe it was fate.

The point is, I've always been in love with you, Seth, and I just never had the nerve

The letter ended there, abruptly. Marquez stared at the words pitching and rolling on the page and tried to make sense of them. Diana and Seth? New Year's?

Diana, in *love* with Seth?

Diana, who was in California with Seth at that very moment.

She'd betrayed Summer during the winter. And she was about to betray her again.

Marquez rubbed her eyes. She threw the letter into the box with a groan. It was too much information. She couldn't cope. She didn't like other people's problems, and these were other people's problems with a vengeance.

What was the etiquette when Friend A stole Friend B's boyfriend and you knew about it? Would it be better to tell Friend B and hurt her? Or to keep your mouth shut, like a sensible human being?

She remembered how grateful Summer had been over spring break when Seth had forgiven her for her indiscretions with Austin. No wonder

Seth had been such a saint! And Diana . . . Diana had actually tried to get Seth and Summer back together. What had that been about? Guilt? No, Diana wasn't the type to feel guilty. She wasn't even really the type to feel, but maybe there was another side to her that Marquez didn't see. After all, Diana had been feeling *something* when she'd written that love letter to Seth.

Marquez clenched her fists. She felt angry for Summer, who'd been lied to and betrayed by Seth and Diana. It wasn't fair. Whatever her faults, at least Summer had tried to make things right with Seth and to keep Austin at bay. Meanwhile, Diana was busy doing her very best to seduce Seth away.

Marquez stood slowly. The world spun for a moment. She needed to clear her head before she decided what to do about this.

Exercise. She would exercise for a while. That was easy, this wasn't. She would ride her bike. She would not go anywhere near the fridge. She would ride longer and faster than she had the day before.

Later she would decide what to do about Diana and Seth and their betrayal. But first things first.

If she rode long enough, she might even burn off the apple she'd had for breakfast.

20

A Picture's Worth a Thousand Lies

"You're not eating anything." Seth pointed to Diana's untouched plate.

"Oh, I'm just not very hungry," Diana said quickly. "Jet lag, I guess."

Seth consulted his watch. "It's dinnertime in Florida." He cocked his head to one side, eyeing her up and down. "I guess this is kind of slumming for you, huh? The guys and I have lunch here every day. The fish is fresh, but I know the place isn't much to look at."

Diana took in the little restaurant, with its tacky marine decor. She hadn't really noticed it until that moment. She'd been too busy looking at Seth. He was even more attractive than she'd remembered, which was saying something. His deep brown eyes always hinted at a smile, and his smile always hinted at some tantalizing and very sexy possibilities.

Or maybe she was just imagining things. Was Seth bored? Uncomfortable? Did he even remember the night that was burned into her own memory?

She stretched out casually, letting her foot just graze his leg under the table. He didn't move. Good. That was a good sign. He would have pulled away if he'd felt really uncomfortable.

Or maybe he just hadn't noticed her foot. Or her.

"You probably would have eaten better if you'd stuck with your mom in Laguna Beach," Seth said.

"But I prefer the company here," Diana replied, sounding more seductive than she'd intended.

Seth took a swig of his Coke. "It would have been cool if Summer could have come along, too."

Oh, yeah. Way cool.

"She was pretty busy," Diana said, "what with job hunting and getting settled in. Seeing old friends, that sort of thing." She ticked off the seconds as she waited for Seth to ask which old friends, but he wasn't biting.

Instead she shifted position a little, her right foot still making contact with Seth's shin. "You know, when I was leaving this morning, Summer and I were talking," Diana said casually. She toyed with a french fry. "And she said you hadn't mentioned that I'd called you to tell you I was coming." She dipped the fry in ketchup, taking her time, then popped it into her mouth delicately, the picture of innocence. "And I was wondering how come."

"How come?" Seth echoed. It was his turn to shift in his seat. "Uh, no reason. You know. I guess it just didn't come up."

"I was starting to worry," Diana said, playing with another french fry, trailing it across her plate, "that you'd told her about what happened between us."

Seth's eyes went wide. "Wh—Why would I do that?" he sputtered. "That was ages ago. It was just a fluke, just a—" He ran out of steam. "No, of course I never told her."

"A fluke." Diana considered the word. "A fun fluke, though, wasn't it?"

A new thought seemed to occur to Seth. "Diana, you didn't *tell* her, did you?"

"Of course not."

"Or tell Marquez, because Marquez would keep her mouth shut for about three seconds flat—"

"No, Seth." Diana reached across the table and took his hand. The feel of his rough fingers made her shiver. "I care about Summer, even if she doesn't . . ."

"Doesn't what?"

Diana pulled her hand away. She had him. Now to reel him in, nice and slow. "Nothing. I was just babbling. Hey, I almost forgot. I brought some pictures of our new apartment. Want to see?"

Seth pursed his lips, still mulling over her words. "Sure."

Diana opened her purse. "Now, keep in mind this is a new camera I was experimenting with, so don't expect miracles. But it'll give you the idea." She withdrew the packet of photos, which she'd carefully organized on the plane trip for maximum impact.

She handed him the first photo. "That's our place from the outside. There's a café and bookstore on the bottom floor and apartments on the upper levels. Cute, huh?"

Seth nodded. "Not bad. Although it's kind of a comedown from your mom's house, isn't it?"

"Well, it doesn't have a Jacuzzi, no. But then, it doesn't have Mallory either." She passed him the next photo. "That's the inside, the day we moved in. I believe I captured Summer and Marquez in all their sweaty glory. Sorry you missed out. Two flights of stairs, no elevator, ninety-six degrees."

Seth gazed fondly at the picture. "Is that Diver in the corner?"

"Yeah. He helped out."

"How's Summer doing with him?"

Diana shrugged. "They're tolerating each other, at least." She handed him another photo.

"That's the backyard view. The pool's a little scuzzy, but you get the idea."

"Who's that? It sort of looks like Summer, but it's hard to tell with all the palms."

Diana checked the photo. "Yeah, that's Summer."

"Who's with her?"

Not too fast. Nice and easy. "I can't tell," Diana said. "Some guy, it looks like."

Seth set the picture aside, unperturbed.

Diana passed him the next picture with calculated nonchalance. "And that's the inside of Jitters, the coffee place downstairs." She added a careful pause. "You know, where Marquez and Austin work."

She waited, flipping through the photos, counting the seconds until Seth absorbed it all.

One one thousand, two one thousand—

"Austin," he repeated. It was barely a whisper.

She had to be careful not to overplay her hand. Diana looked at him, eyes wide, making certain she was conveying her horror. She dropped the photos onto the table with a little gasp—a nice touch, she thought.

"Oh, Seth. Oh, God, I just assumed you knew. . . ."

"He's there, on Coconut Key?"

Diana nodded. She reached out for his hand, but he yanked it away.

"Is that all?" He was seething. She could see

the anger in the tight muscles of his jaw. His words came out like the urgent release of air from a pierced tire. "I mean, he's just there, is that all? Are they . . . is she, you know . . . spending time with him? Being with him?"

Diana didn't answer. She closed her eyes and sighed to make it clear she was far too decent to tell him what he didn't want to hear.

Seth pounded the table. "Tell me, Diana."

Diana rifled through her pictures, as if she didn't know quite what she was looking for. It was right where she'd placed it, at the bottom of the pile.

"Here," she said, pleased and a little shocked when actual tears sprouted in her eyes. She almost hated to hurt Seth this way, but it was, after all, for a greater good.

For a long time he stared at the picture without moving. She was surprised when he suddenly leapt up.

"I have to use the phone," he said, tossing the photo down. Before she could say anything, he was rushing off.

She picked up the picture. The composition was a little off, the focus a little hazy, the palm leaves distracting. Still, she'd managed to nicely capture Summer's rapturous smile as Austin massaged her by the pool.

When the phone rang, Marquez decided to ignore it. Diana's cell phone was on the couch, miles away, and Marquez was on the exercise bike with miles to go. She wasn't sure how long she'd been riding. She knew her legs weren't going very fast, but it didn't seem to matter. She couldn't really feel them anymore. She couldn't feel her body much at all. She was weightless, floating, unattached.

The ringing continued. "Go away," Marquez muttered, but the damn phone kept chirping away incessantly.

At last she climbed slowly off the bike. Her legs nearly gave way, but then she righted herself. Sucking in air, she dragged herself over to the couch and picked up the phone.

"What?" she demanded.

"Marquez? Is that you?"

The voice was fuzzy and faraway, the way Marquez felt inside her head. "Who is this?" she asked, panting.

"It's Seth. Seth Warner. Are you okay? You weren't—I mean, I didn't catch you and Diver in the middle of something—"

"Seth. Imagine that. Is Diana there, too?"

"Um, yeah. We're at a restaurant. Listen, is Summer there? I really need to talk to her."

Fragments of Diana's letter came back to Marquez. She should say something, shouldn't she? Defend Summer? Yell at Seth?

Marquez opened her mouth to speak, but the words had evaporated. Her stomach twisted and lurched. She wondered vaguely if she was going to be sick.

"Marquez?"

Marquez closed her eyes and willed the queasiness away. It had happened before. It was nothing to worry about.

"Marquez, are you there?"

"Seth, Summer isn't here right now. And I have to go."

"But I really need to talk to her."

"Bye, Seth—"

"Just tell me this, Marquez." The edge in Seth's voice finally caught her attention. Was he crying? Or angry? Or both? "Just tell me this. Is she with Austin?"

The dizziness came again, grabbing her hard, shaking the breath from her. The room was dancing past, and she could not keep up.

"Yeah, Seth," Marquez said. She had to lie down, hang up the phone, make Seth go away, make the awful ache in her gut go away. "She's with Austin."

She hung up on him, tossed the phone aside, and tried to stand. Water. A glass of water would be good. No calories.

She was halfway to the sink when her legs gave way and she fell to the floor. Her eyes closed and then, finally, the world stopped its wild dance and stood perfectly still.

21

Decisions, Decisions . . .

Summer dug her toes into the cool, wet sand and sighed. The waves surged and receded in a soothing rhythm, but she didn't feel soothed at all.

Austin sat beside her, close enough for their shoulders to touch.

"Look, I know the lasagna was bad, but was it bad enough to send you into a coma?" he chided.

"Sorry. I guess I haven't been very talkative."

"I know rocks that are more expressive." Austin laced his fingers through hers. "Especially given that this is our second walk of the evening. During the first one you sounded like you had something to say."

"I did. Do."

"But you didn't seem to get around to saying it."

"I'm just . . . trying to sort everything out, Austin." Summer closed her eyes to the silver blanket of stars. "It was hard enough coming to a decision about Carlson today. I came here tonight sure I was going to tell you I never wanted to see you again, but somehow it hasn't been as easy as I'd thought it would be."

"You do know what's standing in your way, don't you?"

"My incredible indecisiveness?"

"No. Our incredible kiss." Austin leaned close. His eyes were bright with moonlight. "Here's the deal, Summer. Seth is the University of Wisconsin. Safe, logical, a good, all-around choice, if a little dull. I, on the other hand, am Carlson. Demanding, difficult, challenging, and a really great kisser."

"I think you may be stretching the analogy."

"You've made one good decision today. Why not go for two?"

Austin cupped her chin in his hands. She felt the same exquisite, tantalizing free fall she always felt when she was close to him. She felt the same irresistible draw, the pull like gravity claiming her.

She stared up at the sky and tried to think of Seth, but her thoughts got lost in the crush of stars. How did he make sense of them, finding pictures in the glittering maze? Why did some people always seem to know just where to look and just what they wanted, when it was so hard for her?

"Where's Venus?" Summer asked.

Austin blinked. "Could we stay on the subject here? Let's stargaze later."

Summer lay back on the sand, one arm under her head. How had she known that it was a good idea to try for Carlson? It wasn't as though there'd been beacons and marching bands and red flags guiding her to the answer. It had been more like a soft glow, a delicate bubble of feeling that said, "This will feel more right than any other choice you can make." And it wasn't as though she still didn't have doubts. Carlson might not take her. Her mom might be furious. Seth most definitely would be furious.

But the little bubble of feeling was still there. Somehow she knew that doing the thing that scared her, the hard thing, was the right thing.

She looked at Austin. He was gazing down at her with obvious longing. He was gorgeous and complicated and wonderful, and she was probably in love with him.

The stars overhead were impossible to know. But Seth had taught her that if you started with a guidepost or two—the Big Dipper, for example—you could learn to navigate them.

Love was a guidepost like that. But when you loved two people, there had to be something more. Summer closed her eyes and searched for a little bubble of feeling, something to hang on to.

Seth had forgiven her once before. Seth had stood by her. Seth had loved her longer. Seth had placed a diamond ring on her finger because he loved her that much.

Loyalty, honor. They were big, important words, but they were there inside her, softly glowing like candles in a far-off window.

She wanted Austin. She loved Austin.

But she loved Seth, too, and she owed him her loyalty in a way she didn't owe Austin. She'd made a vow to Seth. And if she hadn't honored it as well as she should have so far, well, maybe it wasn't too late to try.

"Summer. God, you're beautiful," Austin whispered, but as he brought his lips to hers she at last knew the right thing to say.

"It's time for me to go home," she said. "I'm going to call Seth." She kissed Austin on the cheek, a kiss filled with regret and longing. "I'm sorry, Austin. But that's my choice."

Diana stared out of Seth's bedroom window, watching the ocean come and go. It would be dark soon. She couldn't see any stars yet, but the sky was turning a bruised purple.

"I'm sorry, Seth," she said for what had to be the hundredth time.

After he'd called Marquez, they'd gone back

to Seth's apartment at Diana's suggestion. He'd cried a little, ranted some. Then he'd fallen silent. He'd been lying on his bed staring up at his ceiling, lost in contemplation for way too long. This wasn't working out the way she'd hoped. She hadn't counted on all this messy emotion.

"I don't believe it." Seth sat up, eyes bright, as if he'd come to an obvious conclusion.

"I thought Marquez told you—"

"I don't care." Seth crossed his arms over his chest. "I don't believe it. Summer wouldn't betray me this way. If she's hanging out with Austin, it's because they're friends."

"Maybe," Diana conceded. "But then why didn't she tell you about him?"

"Because . . . because she knew how upset I'd be. She didn't want me worrying when we were so far apart."

His voice had taken on a plaintive, hopeful quality. It made Diana feel pity and frustration. He just wasn't getting it. She was going to have to use her secret weapon, and she didn't want to. Not anymore. It seemed . . . cruel, somehow.

"Summer wouldn't do something like that. She wouldn't," Seth insisted, as much to himself as to Diana.

"Seth," Diana said reasonably, "she already did it once. Have you forgotten spring break?"

"But she told me about that. She's not the

kind of person who would keep a secret—"

"Not like you, you mean?"

Seth looked at her like a wounded animal.

"You never exactly mentioned New Year's to Summer, did you?" Diana added.

Seth closed his eyes and sighed deeply. "I know. I know. I'm a hypocrite."

"Well, then, so am I." Diana went over to the bed and sat beside him. Not too close, but close enough. She touched his hand.

"I don't regret what happened between us, Seth. Do you?"

Seth stared through her as if she were a pane of glass. He didn't answer.

"She wouldn't do it," he said at last. "We were engaged, Diana. She was wearing my ring."

Diana took a long, slow breath. "I want you to know something, Seth. I didn't want to do this. I didn't want to come here and tell you these things. But in my heart, I knew you deserved the truth. You deserve a whole lot better than this. A whole lot better."

She reached for her purse. Slowly she unzipped the little pouch.

When she took out the ring and held it in the air, Seth didn't react. He just stared at it, mesmerized, as if she'd performed a fantastic, impossible magic trick.

"She hasn't worn it for a long time, Seth," Diana whispered.

Slowly he pulled his gaze from the ring to Diana. His eyes were hard and dark.

"You certainly came prepared," he said. "You brought everything but fingerprints, Diana. 'Gee whiz, Seth, didn't Summer mention Austin?' Why'd you even bother with the innocent act? Why not just trot out the evidence like the FBI?"

Diana looked away. "I thought you liked innocent," she said. "It always worked for Summer."

Seth yanked the ring from her grasp and threw it across the room. In one swift move he pulled Diana down on top of him.

She could still hear the ring rolling slowly across the floor as they began to kiss.

If you've enjoyed MAKING WAVES
you'll love MAKING OUT!

MAKING OUT is a brilliant series about a bunch of teenagers who've grown up together on a tiny island. They think they know everything about one another . . . but they're only just beginning to find out the truth.

1. Zoey fools around
2. Jake finds out
3. Nina won't tell
4. Ben's in love
5. Claire gets caught
6. What Zoey saw
7. Lucas gets hurt
8. Aisha goes wild
9. Zoey plays games
10. Nina shapes up
11. Ben takes a chance
12. Claire can't lose
13. Don't tell Zoey
14. Aaron lets go
15. Who loves Kate?
16. Lara gets even
17. Two-timing Aisha